ALSO BY L.M. BROWN

Debris
Treading the Uneven Road

Were We Awake

L. M. Brown

Fomite
Burlington, VT

ISBN-13: 978-1-947917-33-0
Library of Congress Control Number: 2019949176
Fomite
58 Peru Street
Burlington, VT 05401

For My Parents
Bill and Mary

No man can know where he is going unless he knows exactly where he has been and exactly how he arrived at his present place.
Maya Angelou

it is good we are dreaming—
It would hurt us—were we awake—
Emily Dickinson

CONTENTS

COMMUNION

IN THE CLASSROOM, the children's voices were often lost amidst the high pitched drills of the quarry. On the morning of the accident, a sudden silence brought the teacher to the window under the children's watchful gaze. Many of them had fathers working in the quarry. Raymond's father worked with the digger. Alby's father put the explosives into the holes made in the rock and set off the blasts that occurred twice a week. Raymond's Da, Mr. Hurley, was a large man with wide shoulders and a broad back and arms that could hold Raymond up until his mother started shouting at him to let him down. Alby's Da, Mr. Clancy was thin; the only broadness being his forehead that had become more prominent since his hair had started to recede. Mr. Hurley was stronger, but Alby's Da was quicker, and he had a more dangerous job since he had to crawl into the quarry holes and blow them up to loosen the larger rocks that Mr. Hurley had to pick up.

The men's families lived in a housing estate that was walking distance from the quarry and consisted of small houses, grouped in twos with wooden fences and side paths leading to the back. In the evening, the children would run out to greet their fathers when the men came home with dust and grime on their faces.

There was not a single snigger or whisper while the teacher remained at the window. She didn't smile when she finally moved away. The children were rigid in their seats, waiting for her to say, "Alright children," in her soft easy voice, but without saying a word, she went to the board and started to write addition and subtraction for the children to take down.

The silence made Alby restless. His legs started to jiggle under his desk, and for once the teacher didn't ask him to stay still. Raymond was on the other side of the class by the window, but he wasn't looking out. He was taking down the sums with a look of concentration. His dark hair fell over his eyes each time he looked at his copy book. Alby wanted to be where Raymond was; an arm's reach from the window. Alby would have liked to press his face against the glass, and then he might hear something from outside. Raymond didn't glance about the window, and he didn't seem to care about the silence either.

"Alby," the teacher said.

He saw her standing with arms crossed and frowning. She might have said something else, only it was at that moment that the quiet was broken by the sirens. The fall of her face startled Alby.

This time when the teacher ran to the window, the children ran after her and pushed each other out of the way to get to the glass. Alby stuck at the back fought to press between Sinead and Mary, but they closed their borders, and refused to be parted. Small and thin, like his father, Alby couldn't get by Hazel Thompson or Philip Kelby either and he was not at the window when the ambulance went by.

"Alright, back to your seats," the teacher said when the ambulance disappeared and the sirens had grown faint. The children dispersed, like leaves blown in the wind, to leave Raymond alone in the middle of the window at the perfect focal point, until the teacher said. "That means you too Raymond Hurley."

Alby was half-way through his sums. Others had finished a long time before and were given 'Ann and Barry' books to read. Raymond had been one of the first to put up his hand and say he was done. "Good," the teacher said, and gave him a book that Raymond would fly through, but Alby wouldn't. He preferred the pictures to the words.

She strolled around the class looking over the children's shoulders at their work.

"Is that all you've done?" she said to Alby, and he wanted to tell her it wasn't his fault. Every time she stopped to look where the ambulance had gone, he couldn't take his eyes off her. She seemed sad. She was never usually sad and he wondered what she was looking for. Only when she pulled her gaze back to the classroom could he concentrate on work.

When the knock came, twenty-two children sat upright in their seats. They saw the teacher's hand go to her mouth and her reluctance to go to the door. Sinead Murphy, who cried when she made a mistake or when she couldn't find her pencil, started to whimper, but the teacher didn't tell her that she shouldn't worry or that everything would be okay.

Alby couldn't see who it was. There was a murmur and the teacher nodded. She took a deep breath, before she turned towards the class. The children leaned forward. Alby was half-standing with the hope that for once he would be the one picked. The teacher's gaze would find him and then she'd smile and say his name and everyone in the class including Raymond would want to be him, but she didn't look at him.

"Raymond," she said.

Alby's mother was waiting for him outside the school. Usually he walked home with Raymond, and their mother's took turns collecting them. It was Mrs. Hurley's turn today. Alby had been hoping she would come with Raymond because Mrs. Hurley would let them play for a while in the school grounds, or take them to the slip of road near the quarry that led to the bay. Alby's mother was usually too tired after working in the bar at night.

His mother was talking to the women when he ran out the gate, and he had to stand still while they spoke softly above him.

The ambulance was forgotten, and the quiet that had come from the quarry all day wasn't as important as Raymond's absence.

"Where's Raymond?" he asked, when his mother had finally stopped whispering. His mother bent down to him, and he saw her eyes were red and sore looking. He had an urge to touch her face, but he kept his hands by his side while she told him that Raymond was at home with his Mammy. Alby would have asked why, only he was afraid that his mother might pull him in for a hug like she used to do in the mornings. He would have been embarrassed with Sinead beside him. He nodded and said okay, before his mother got the chance.

She said, "Stop Alby," when he got to the side of the road, though there were no lorries coming or going from the quarry. The only cars in sight were parked waiting for children.

There were three cars outside Raymond's house. Alby expected Raymond to appear at the front door. Even when he was sick with the mumps, Raymond used to stand in his pajamas tucked between the net curtain and the glass, to wave at Alby coming home. But today, the net curtain stayed still.

Inside his house, Alby smelled the smoke straight away. It was coming from the kitchen, and he glanced at his mother who was busy taking off her coat and hanging it up on the hanger by the door. She hated his father smoking inside. Sometimes when it was raining he was allowed to stand at the back door and blow the smoke out, but then the kitchen door stayed closed so the smoke wouldn't reach the rest of the house. Alby imagined the smoke might turn at the end of the stairs and drift upwards to their rooms to sneak under beds because his mother said it went into every room. She said that it was not good for children to be in a smoker's house.

His mother smiled at Alby and told him to take off his jacket. But Alby didn't want to. He wanted to go across the road to Raymond's house and see why the cars were parked outside and why Raymond had been picked above everyone else to go home early.

"I want to go outside," he said. His mother was still dressed in her 'around the house' pants as she called them and an old t-shirt.

"Not today, Alby. We need to be quiet today."

"Why?"

But she was already walking towards the smoky kitchen. He followed her and at the kitchen door he felt a sensation in his stomach, not unlike when the jack-in-the-box jumped out last Christmas and gave him a fright. He'd cried then, though he didn't cry while he stared at his father who was sitting at the kitchen table. He was still in his work clothes. His jeans were dusty and grimy, and his boots had made marks on the floor. His hands were filthy, and Alby couldn't remember a time when his father was allowed wear his boots inside or sit at the table without changing, nor could Alby remember a time when his father was home before him. His father's hands were shaking. A strange sound came from him and scared Alby. Alby's mother rested a hand on Alby's father's back. She asked if he was okay and Alby's father shook his head and said no, he was not okay. "I can't get it out of my head."

He stamped his cigarette out on a plate that held an untouched sandwich. His shoulders were quivering. And Alby's mother remembered her son and said, "Alby go put on the telly. I'll bring you something to eat in a minute."

His father was still folded up on the chair. Smoke rose from the plate, and Alby said he didn't want to watch television. He wanted to go outside.

"I already told you, there's no going outside today."

Alby's eyes were stinging from the smoke. He wanted his father to look at him and smile, to stop making those noises.

"I want to see Raymond."

Usually after school, Alby would dump his bag by the door and grab an apple or a piece of bread before darting out into the street. It was a competition to see who could get back onto the street first, and Alby hated that Raymond might have seen his arrival and was already standing on the curb.

"Please Alby," his mother said, and it was the same voice she used when she wanted to sleep during the day and he needed to be quiet.

"What if Raymond's outside?"

"Alby!" his father's loud voice startled Alby, and he was already starting to cry before he saw the dirty streaks on his father's face and his red eyes, which were worse than Alby's mother's.

"Raymond's not going to be outside today. Now do as you're bloody told and put on the telly!"

Alby's mother went to him and hugged him, before unzipping his jacket and taking it off. She said she'd make a sandwich and bring it into him and if he stopped crying he'd get a surprise, and he wanted to stop crying, but it was hard.

"Go on now," she said and gave him a light push so he stumbled back into the hallway. He didn't move, but she had already turned away from him.

"Jim, we need to go over to them," she said to her husband.

Alby's father shook his head. "I keep seeing him. Every time I blink it's there. I can't face them with that." He buried his face in his hands.

The Hurley's side gate was open, and there was a white sheet on their clothes line. Every now and again, it was lifted by the wind to give a brief flutter before it fell. Alby saw Hazel Thompson's father in the back garden. He had the same curly hair as his daughter and was speaking to another man who wore a cap. The man in the cap threw his cigarette on the ground and walked away, to leave Hazel Thompson's father standing rigid and looking at something in the garden and Alby wondered what he was looking at. A woman appeared, and Alby knew it was Hazel's mother, because he saw her at mass with Hazel every Sunday. The last time, Hazel's mother had gone to Raymond's house was a few weeks ago when Raymond's parents had a party for Raymond, and Alby had been there too and not stuck at home watching everyone through the window. He imagined Hazel inside that house with Raymond, the two eating cakes piled with cream, just like last time. There was a big clown at the party, too, who'd come down all the way from Dublin, and Raymond's father did some card tricks and his mother shook with laughter, and it wasn't fair that Hazel was in Raymond's house, and Alby wasn't.

A car pulled up in front of the house, and Alby watched the priest emerge. Kneeling on the couch with his belly pressed up against the back, it was hard for Alby to sit still. There was no one out on the street today. No screeches of his friends playing, and no frustrated cries from Sinead, who lived a few doors down and spent half her time with her finger in her mouth, and the other half crying, which meant even Sinead Murphy, who Raymond called a baby, was in the house across the road.

A plate with half a sandwich was on the floor by the couch. Beside this was a bowl that had not a trace of ice cream because Alby had licked it clean while watching Dempsey's Den. It was hard to concentrate on the TV, with the people going in and out of Raymond's house and the quiet outside, which was making him restless.

He heard the kitchen door open and the shuffle of his father's steps. His father stopped at the living room door. His face was still dirty and his hair was pulled tight off his face.

"I'm sorry for shouting," he said.

Alby felt like crying, though he wasn't sure why. Something about his father made him sad, not just the dirty clothes or streaked face. He'd stopped just outside the door, as if he couldn't come into the room and it made Alby think of the game where Alby and Raymond couldn't step on the cracks of the pavement. For his father, the room was the crack. Alby felt lonelier than he had for the last half hour while he'd watched the house across the road, and he wished his father would go away and stop confusing him.

"There was an accident in the quarry," his father said. He paused and blew out air. "Raymond's daddy," he said. He shook his head and looked towards the ceiling and said, "Jesus."

"Jim, you need to shower," Alby's mother was beside his father. and he was nodding without looking at anyone and saying okay, okay. He tried to smile at Alby, but Alby's mother was easing him away from the door, and Alby felt the knot tighten in his belly.

"I don't know what I'm at," his father said, "I can't think straight, Sara."

And his mother said, "I know, come on now."

She led her husband upstairs while Alby looked at the house across the road. He waited until his mother and father were upstairs before he slipped off the couch. When he heard the shower go on, he opened his front door and darted outside and ran across the road.

Raymond's back garden was empty, and Alby's shout for Raymond got caught in his throat when he stood at the open back door and stared into the gloomy kitchen. Hazel's parents were gone. Mrs. Hurley sat at the table beside the priest. Raymond was sitting on the armchair by the range with his head down, and an elderly neighbor Ester had her arm around him. At the party, Mr. Hurley had sat on that armchair while he showed them card tricks. There was no laughter now. only the sound of the priest's soft voice and the kettle starting to boil. Through the darkness, Alby saw Ester rise to walk to the kettle. She stalled when she saw him. "Alby, you need to go home," she said.

Raymond looked up to show a face swollen from crying, but he didn't say that it was okay for Alby to come in. The priest grew quiet. Alby wanted to ask where Mr. Hurley was. He wanted to tell Raymond that he shouldn't be sitting in his father's chair, but he was afraid to ask, and the quiet that surrounded the kitchen made Alby want to cry. He'd remember for years to come his friend's small body rising from his seat and moving through that still awful silence to take hold of his hand and lead him home across the quiet street.

His mother stood at the door watching them with tears in her eyes. She nodded to Raymond, when she had her son beside her, and said in a soft voice, "Raymond," but nothing else came from her, and he was walking away. In the house, Alby heard his father's movements upstairs, and his mother bent down to face him with a tight grip firm on his arms. He didn't cry when his mother said, "You shouldn't have left the house." He cried when she hugged him.

Hidden

Clouds drifted low in the sky and sent shadows over the furniture, and the girl at the table. She was not a big girl, but wide-shouldered like her mother with curly hair falling around her face. The clock ticking felt loud today and an empty mug was in front of her. A plate held crumbs and a half slice of toast. She couldn't eat much this morning.

"Haz?" Her aunt called from the room beside the kitchen.

When Hazel heard a shuffle coming from there, she stood quickly and said she was going outside. The shuffling stopped and Hazel felt guilty for not wanting to sit in that room today. She'd planned to have breakfast with her aunt, but she hadn't accounted for the fear. Fear was different from nerves. The nerves made her laugh and act stupid during the last few days. The fear made her want to hide. Earlier, Hazel had said good morning to her aunt, and then she'd said that she needed to do some things and would be back later. Her aunt's face had fallen because they'd planned this morning together. It was a milestone in Hazel's life. Her aunt liked talking about milestones. When Hazel was getting her Holy Communion and Confirmation, she saw milestones as part of the bridge to adulthood. Now she believed they were turning points, and she was supposed to share it with her aunt, but Hazel couldn't share the waiting. The waiting was too personal.

She'd gone as far as taking the phone of the hook in case Sinead or Maeve might call with news about their offerings. They lived two miles away in the housing estate in the village, so the post would come to them first, and though Hazel had said she'd phone once she knew, Maeve was not known for her patience. It would be just like her to phone to say, well? Hazel couldn't stand the idea. She'd thought of her mother's friend, June, in the house next door when she put the phone face down and felt some guilt. June was as nervous as Hazel the last few days, and she was bad at hiding it. Sometimes June reminded Hazel of a chicken running around the place, not for the running, but the way she'd sit and wave her hands, and say oh my gosh, and then grow still again. June was older than Hazel's mother and very thin, which was another reason she made Hazel think of a chicken.

Hazel had told June not to come near the house, until at least ten minutes after the postman, which wasn't taken too lightly by June, since she helped Hazel's mother in the garden during the summer and they shadowed each other. Hazel thought of them as a more serious Laurel and Hardy. Her mother was the stockier of the two, though Hazel would never voice this to anyone, not even to Sinead and Maeve, because she'd hate her mother hearing.

Outside it was a blustery day, and she was immediately cold though it was still summer and she wore jeans and a sweater. The sea crashed on the rocks below her. The sea was a darker more forceful grey than the sky. Hazel was often amazed by all the different shades of grey, though the rocks had a blue tint to them and patches of white. Movement by the rocks caught Hazel's eyes, and her fears were replaced by disbelief. She knew who it was, even as she went to the back of the house to the raised bed and the green house. There, she heard banging from her father's shed. Sometimes, if she listened carefully, she'd hear Lorcan's saw going back and forth on the wood. To her, it was the same sound as a panting dog. It was a game at one time, to try and guess what tool he was using from the noises emitted. Now, she paid little heed to it, though she knew he would stop soon and come to find her if she did not run to him. He'd give her ten minutes after the postman, just as she'd asked.

Her mother was not at her raised beds, nor was she in the green house. Although, Hazel knew she would not be there, it still shocked her. The postman was starting down her road and Hazel had forgotten him in her distress. How could her mother leave? From the front of the garden, she saw the figure bend and rise again. Her mother was collecting seaweed. Behind Hazel, there was a crunch of tires. Hazel watched the figure bend and forgot to check the time.

She would have seen it was 10:32, if she'd looked. If

she'd listened, she would have heard the silence that was broken by the crashing of the waves, and the cawing of a seagull. She would have known that her father heard the postman and was standing by the shed door watching his daughter. She couldn't turn around.

"There's a letter for you," the postman said.

His name was Tom, and he was a small man with a long chin and a habit of keeping his cap low on his head, which made Hazel think of the robbers in the cartoons she used to watch as a kid. Her mother was a figure drifting on the sand. Hazel felt her out there, as she went towards the letter. She managed to smile when Tom said good luck.

He would have known the importance of the day. The whole country had people like her waiting to see if they got into college. She opened the letter and saw the movement at the door of the shed. Her father had stepped out. Her aunt might have gone to the kitchen window on her crutches, but Hazel didn't look. She read the letter and whooped and screamed and felt as light as a feather when she ran to her Dad. "I got in, I got in. I'm going to Galway."

June was coming through the gate, when Hazel finished hugging her Dad. June might have heard Hazel's screams, though Hazel would learn later that she'd asked Tom if there was anything for Hazel. "You cheater," Hazel said, and June said she couldn't help it. She was going mad waiting around. This was after Hazel had run into her aunt Bevin's room. Her aunt had not gotten up to look out the window. She was propped up in her armchair. Sunlight fell on her blonde hair and pale skin. A book lay face down on her knee, and her foot was resting on a stool. Hazel never saw the foot anymore. She never thought of her aunt as anything but beautiful, with her small face and lovely skin.

"I'm going to be a midwife," Hazel said.

She hugged her aunt and helped her up, so they could celebrate with a cake the aunt had baked yesterday.

It was June who asked, "Where's Evelyn?"

Hazel was getting plates down, and said her mother was at the beach.

"She gets something in her head and that's it, no bloody patience," June said. Hazel was surprised at her anger, while her father shrugged the absence off and said that Evelyn would have lost all track of time.

"Yeah well, I'll get her," June said.

Hazel watched June storm out, and was struck by a sudden sorrow from her leaving. There was a sense of imbalance and discomfort in the silence that issued from the three people left in the room. She would have liked to follow June and watch her trek down the stony path to the figure of her mother. She would have seen the two women standing close together, and the seconds of stillness before her mother's arms went around June and they held each other, and Hazel would have known that her mother had not forgotten. The lingering around the house had been too much for her. She'd chosen to leave and collect seaweed and wait to be called.

Hazel was at the table with her cake and tea when her mother came in and brought the smell of the sea and grains of sand that would take days to sweep up fully. Her dark hair was pulled back, and she looked surprised when she stepped into the room as though she had not expected to have anyone there. Her gaze fell on Hazel, who had an urge to spring from the chair and run to her mother. Hazel had always loved her mother's smile for the way it opened up her face and made her look younger.

Her mother said, "Where's the whiskey? We need a drop to celebrate."

The aunt laughed and said it wasn't even 11 o clock and Evelyn said, "So bloody what, we need to mark this occasion, a drop won't kill us." So it was settled, because Evelyn had a way of settling things.

They had their cake and their shot of whiskey, all except Lorcan, who was going back to the shed and didn't want to chance losing a limb or messing up the cabinet he'd nearly finished making. He left the women to talk about Hazel being a midwife and helping women like her mother who had not wanted to give birth in the hospital.

"You should have been born right here and the sea should have been your first sound," her mother said enough to make Hazel start to imagine it.

She sat between her mother and her aunt, while June stood by the sink, and it hit Hazel that she was leaving, though it might have been the whiskey that hit her too. "A drop more than the others," is what June had said with a wink, and all of a sudden Hazel was crying and saying that she didn't want to leave.

"No one wants to leave, right Bevin?" Hazel's mother said.

Bevin glanced at her sister and she might have reddened. There was discomfort there, a mild silence, but Bevin managed to smile and say, "That's right, but some of us have to, at least for a while."

Later, after the phone calls with her friends, and the screaming down the line, because Sinead had gotten an offer for business in Galway and Maeve an offer for Arts in Galway, and the disprin to help with Hazel's headache, she knocked on her aunt's bedroom door at the back of the kitchen. The window looked out to the sea and under this was an armchair where her aunt loved to sit. Beyond the aunts bedroom was her bathroom, which was the last room built onto the house six years ago when Bevin's arthritis started to worsen.

Her leg was lifted up on the stool and a blanket had been thrown over her foot. As a child, Hazel had been in awe of her twisted foot with the curled toes.

"Bad foot," she used to say. One day, her mother told her that a witch had cursed the foot. Hazel had run into the room and before Bevin knew what was going on she'd pulled the blanket off her and kissed it. This made Evelyn laugh in the re-telling, until Bevin and Hazel asked her to stop. It was a story neither of them liked—Bevin because of the shock the child had given her when she'd run in and grabbed the blanket and Hazel because of the helplessness she'd felt with the foot did not miraculously heal.

"Are you getting hungry? Should I make dinner early?" Bevin asked.

The day had grown duller and Bevin's face was in shadow.

The room seemed too dark, though in the next instant there was a ray of light. A cloud moved by the sun and Hazel realized her aunt had been sleeping. She said no, she wasn't hungry. She didn't bother say that she was old enough to fix something to eat if she needed. Bevin didn't like to hear that. In the last years, she rested her leg on a chair while she cooked because it was painful to stand too long.

Bevin was young, five years Evelyn's junior.

"What is it?" Bevin asked. She'd sat up and turned the lamp on.

Hazel shrugged and sat on the bed. She said, "You stayed to mind me."

There was the distant sound of the sea. Bevin nodded and said, "Yes, that was part of it." She seemed to be waiting. Her gaze was soft and expectant and Hazel remembered every afternoon running straight for this room with Bevin at the kitchen table doing her homework, while her mother worked outside. She wanted to ask what Bevin would do now, but sensed the wrongness in it. "Maybe I will eat something," she said instead.

When Evelyn and Lorcan bought the land and the shell of the house in 1972, they didn't know she was pregnant. For the first year they lived in a caravan on the site. There were photos of them sitting on the couches in the caravan holding playing cards and smiling towards the camera and of Evelyn sitting on the steps by the caravan door sticking out her tongue, and all the while her belly was growing and her face was getting rounder. There was a picture of her standing inside the caravan by the table. She was talking to the seated Lorcan who was looking up at her, and she was nearly the width of the caravan. Lorcan was tall and skinny, and there were photos of him stepping barefoot out of the caravan with his hand to his face blocking the sun, or sawing wood in the open space. June had taken the photos of them. They'd met her after they bought the land. She taught Irish dancing in national schools, and she was Evelyn and Lorcan's chronicler. Without her, there might have been no evidence of what the house had been like when they arrived, with the broken walls and windows, the rubble on the ground and the sky visible through the roof. Evelyn helped with the building, but Lorcan refused to let her work after her seventh month. She took to walking the beach then. There were photos of her in a smock and threading down in bare feet with her hands on her bulging stomach and her hair falling down one side of her face.

The photos of June never have her looking at the camera. She was at the wall staring out at the beach with a worried look on her face, or standing near the site with Evelyn, her head thrown back in laughter, while Evelyn was watching her with a smile. Another showed them sitting by an open fire, where they used to cook in the good weather. Lorcan often told Hazel that her mother wasn't meant to be kept within walls. He said she nearly went mad in the caravan for the lack of space. Some mornings, he'd wake and find her asleep outside.

When Hazel was born at the end of May, they bought a

tent because a restless Hazel would keep Lorcan up and that couldn't happen if they wanted to be in the house by the end of the summer. June's camera caught Evelyn's head peeking out of the tent, or her sitting by the entrance-way breastfeeding. Evelyn said the sounds of the sea often lulled Hazel back to sleep and once they were in the house, Hazel had nights where she would not settle until Evelyn brought her outside to the stars and the waves.

Hazel loved those photos, seeing how it all started and how young her parents were. Her final weeks in the house, she looked at them whenever she got a chance. She preferred to do it when she knew she wouldn't be interrupted because the images saddened her with the thought of leaving. During this time, while she sat with Bevin, or had dinner with her family, there was a sense of things left unsaid. It was a relief to get away to Galway with Sinead and Maeve to look for a house to rent together. But when she finally moved that September, Hazel couldn't settle.

She thought of her mother and Bevin often, and with a nostalgia that scared her, as if they were a part of a past she would never get back to again. She knew she was waiting for the phone call from Bevin to say she was leaving. Bevin was only twenty-one when she'd arrived at her sister's house. There'd been a near marriage. Bevin had spoken about it once when Hazel was around twelve and starting to realize that her aunt must have had a life outside their house; a near marriage that was called off, and Hazel was sure it was the man because Bevin said she didn't want to speak of it again. So

Bevin had gone to her sister and she'd stayed to help with Hazel while they were finishing the house and then to help while Evelyn started to build raised beds, and talk about organic farming when no one knew what it was.

Hazel had never imagined her life without her aunt, and now she imagined Bevin's life without her, alone while Lorcan and Evelyn worked. How lonely was she staring out at the sea? Or working in the kitchen cooking their meals? Hazel hated the thought of Bevin giving so much to Hazel and then being left behind and the more she thought of her mother's comment, the crueler it seemed.

"No one wants to leave, right Bevin?"

Bevin had managed to smile, but not before showing her discomfort with the insinuation that it was time to leave. Wasn't that what her mother meant? Sinead didn't think so. She was a chubby girl with short hair and a tendency to cry over the slightest thing. She sat across from Hazel at the kitchen table, while Maeve fried eggs. Maeve was slender with straight hair that was always in a ponytail. She could have been taken for a fourteen-year-old.

"Your mother wouldn't kick her out," Sinead insisted.

Hazel said it wasn't a matter of getting kicked out. It was a matter of not needing to be there anymore.

"I couldn't imagine your aunt not there." Sinead liked to go into Bevin's room and talk with her. She'd said once that there was a Victorian feel to the whole thing, and Hazel said, "What, you mean the cripple being hidden away?"

Sinead was the romantic, Maeve the pragmatist. "If you're

so worried about it," she said, when she'd given the girls their eggs, and sat down. "Just go home and find out."

Hazel said that was pointless because she would get home and no-one would say anything.

"Usually, it's the parents who have a hard time when the kids go to college, not the kids." Maeve was the youngest of five, and her mother had bawled when she brought her to Galway. Maeve had grown to dislike her weekly phone calls, because of her mother's sighs and lamentations that her house was too quiet.

Hazel had grown to dislike her calls home too, because she was never able to ask what she wanted. "Are you okay Bevin?" got caught in her throat and she'd leave the phone box feeling desolate and angry.

It was Maeve's idea to surprise them with a visit. If no one knew she was coming, they couldn't prepare themselves. And if Bevin was lonely and lost, Hazel would know the first instance of seeing her. The surprise could make Bevin cry and open up, and Hazel would get to see her mother unguarded too. Hazel had laughed at this thought. She said her mother was never unguarded. Even when she stopped in the garden to look out at the sea, her face was closed and secretive. Still she agreed a surprise visit was the only thing to do.

Hazel phoned every Saturday morning, but it was decided that she would phone on Friday and tell them that she would be busy in the morning.

She would get the 9 o'clock bus to the village, and then ring a taxi from the phone box on Main Street, to take her the couple of miles home. She would tell the driver to stop just after June's house to reduce the risk of being seen by her. Bevin would not hear the car, and she would have no opportunity to prepare herself. Even if she didn't cry, which Sinead was convinced she would, Hazel could simply say. "I was worried about you."

"And what if I'm right, what then?" she asked.

The girls glanced at each other and shrugged.

It was October and a clear morning. For once, Hazel didn't mind the regular stops in towns along the way, or the fifteen minutes spent in Knock, watching the pilgrims, mostly aged and in groups, walk to church. She thought of her conversation with Bevin last night. She'd sounded surprised with the call and then concerned. Hazel assured her that everything was okay and a change of schedule meant she couldn't phone tomorrow. Bevin had offered to get Lorcan, but she'd said nothing about Evelyn.

Hazel phoned for the taxi from the phone box, and was thankful she saw no-one she recognized. The streets were quiet on that Saturday when she drove out of village and towards the sea. June's house was still and quiet. The breeze had turned chilly, but the sky was clear of clouds. A few sheep grazed in the fields beside her and in the distance she could hear the cars from the main road. The low hum faded as she walked and was replaced by the loose stones under her feet.

No sound came from the shed, which surprised Hazel since it was a good hour after lunch. A shovel had been thrown onto the raised bed, and it made Hazel's discomfort grow. Her mouth had dried halfway through the taxi ride, and she wished she'd brought water. Even with the chill breeze, she felt a little hot. The murmur of the sea eased her, and she stopped to look towards it. She saw the two figures then. They were down by the shore, and she knew her mother was one of them because she wore her dark shawl that she liked to wrap around her when she walked. The other figure she thought must be her father.

"You need to surprise her," Maeve had said, "No shouting, hello, it's me."

Hazel thought of that as she opened the back door and knew Maeve was right in saying that Hazel would feel uncomfortable in her stealth.

The noise should have stopped her from continuing, but she heard the low moan and did not hear it at the same time. The second moan reached her as a sob. Hazel had an image of her aunt crying alone, and her heart had grown twice the size by the time she'd reached the bedroom door. The door opened to a darkened room. The curtains were pulled and a slice of light came from the gap between them and still Hazel didn't think of it. How could she? She'd tell Maeve and Sinead, how could she have imagined such a thing? Then there was gasp and a shuffle, a flash of bare skin amid the shadows and forms and her aunt's, "Oh my God!"

Hazel saw her father's bare shoulder, and she heard him say, "Jesus."

Hazel was frozen with shock, and then all of a sudden she was running through the kitchen and knocking over a chair.

Her mother was a dot on the beach. June must have been with her. They'd gone for a walk, but they were so close when her father went to her aunt. To think of it was unbearable. Hazel ran through the garden and ignored his call. She was gasping for breath, when she scampered through the gate and up the road, but it was impossible to stop. She heard her father's car start and didn't turn around. He parked up the road ahead of her and got out. She kept walking. She would not look at his face when he pleaded with her to listen. His boots were unlaced and his jeans dirty from work, and she thought she was looking at something she didn't know, something new to her. Nothing was familiar, as if the world she knew had slid away and she was noticing what lay underneath it. His voice was not her father's. She didn't want to think of the bodies she'd seen, and the way her aunt had hidden her face, but it came back in flashes, and made her sluggish and fired up at the same time. She wanted to lie on the ground and scream and shout, to pull the hair from her head and feel something other than the confusion. He stopped in front of her. She saw the thinness of him under the t-shirt, but she could not stop walking. It was impossible to face him or everything that she was feeling. She tried to walk around him, but he held her arm. She didn't know she was going to hit him, until she felt the hardness of him. She was hitting him again and again and screaming for him to get away. She was crying and he didn't touch her again. He said, "Haz, please."

There would be questions later that she wished she'd asked. Back in the house in Galway, curled up in her bed, she'd wonder if her mother knew, and if that was why she spent so much time outside. And she'd think that she couldn't know. The fact of having to tell Evelyn was what kept her father on that narrow road staring helplessly after Hazel. He had not moved by the time she got to the main road that led to the village. She'd glanced back to see him standing still watching after her. Two miles she walked with her head down afraid to look around her and see anyone she knew. Two miles and she had the sense that her father had not moved, that when she finally sat on the bus and leaned her head on the window he was still standing on the road.

The girls pleaded with Hazel to tell them what happened. That Saturday night, they'd been out and came home late to find her crying in her bedroom. Every time, she closed her eyes, she saw the opening of that bedroom door and the forms on the bed. She wouldn't tell them because she couldn't speak of it. The shame was greater than the anger, though the girls persisted and in the middle of the week, after fits of crying and shouting, she finally told them what she'd seen. "Jesus Christ," Maeve said, "How could they do that?"

"What are you going to do?" Sinead asked.

Hazel hadn't thought of her doing anything.

"Are you going to tell your mother?"

Hazel said she was never going back to that house.

Maeve phoned Hazel's house the following Friday to say that Hazel was fine, as in not dead, but not great either. Bevin came to the phone. Maeve told Bevin that Hazel was okay, but she would not phone the house ever again. Bevin sighed into the phone. She said she needed to talk to Hazel because she needed to explain, and Maeve said it was a bit late for that. She asked if Evelyn knew. There was a drawn out silence at the other end.

Bevin said, "Hazel needs to ask me that."

After two weeks of silence, a letter came from Bevin. Hazel recognized the writing, and remembered all those evenings at the kitchen table when Bevin helped her with her homework, and the times Hazel had run into Bevin's room crying over some hurt. Hazel had thought her aunt iridescent, but there was a taint to her memories now; a dark two-headed shape that she couldn't get rid of. She couldn't open the letter and sent it back unopened.

That week, Hazel stepped out of her house and saw her mother parked across the street. It was impossible for Hazel to understand all her feelings. Anger was there, but there was also a resigned sympathy, as if the woman she was seeing was someone distant to her. Her mother was dressed in her usual dark clothes and her hair was pulled back. Her head was bent and for a moment, Hazel thought she was crying, but she was too still for that. Her hands were gripping the steering wheel. Hazel had never seen her mother so immobile, so pre-occupied and unsure. During the previous weeks, Hazel had suffered through the realization that her mother must have known about her husband and Bevin. Otherwise, she would have written or driven up, demanding to know why Hazel hadn't phoned or come home for her scheduled visit. Her mother looked towards the house, and Hazel darted inside and ran to her bedroom upstairs. After a time, she saw her mother get out of the car. The silence of the house reverberated through Hazel. There was no ring of the doorbell or knock and a glance showed her mother walking back to the car. In the hallway, there was an envelope and Hazel sat on the bottom stair and opened it to find the photos she had spent the summer looking at. They weren't all there, just a few; her mother sitting by the opening of the tent breastfeeding; her father coming out of the caravan and not looking at the camera; June and Evelyn sitting around the fire laughing; Evelyn treading to the beach and Bevin standing at the doorway of the house, smiling shyly.

A note was with the photos.

Bevin said you looked at these photos a lot during the summer and I thought I should bring some to you. I didn't tell your father or Bevin that I was coming to see you. They would have wanted to come and I didn't think you'd want that. I didn't think that you wouldn't want to talk to me until I saw you run back into the house. I'm so sorry. I've been sitting here trying to figure out what to say and that is the only thing I've come up with. I know it's not enough. Mom.

It hurt to see the images. The thought of what she'd walked into had gotten worse as time progressed. She remembered the darkened gloom of it and the strange noises, and had started to forget those people any other way and now her mother was in that room with them. She'd known what was happening. *They would have wanted to come....*There was nothing about her mother's pain or shock or anger, nothing, but sympathy towards her father. Hazel sent the photos back and tore up the note.

During her loneliest times, when the girls went home for weekends, Hazel wandered the promenade in Salthill where she had to share the sea with the joggers and walkers and the purr of traffic. She'd think of her stretch of sea at home, and she'd wish she'd kept the note so she could read it and strengthen her resolve to stay away. During Christmas vacation, she phoned her house and Bevin answered and said hello. Hazel recognized the voice and didn't recognize it at the same time. It drifted to her and confused her, and in the phone box with the chatter of the street reaching her, she'd wonder what had brought her to dial the number. She had nothing to say.

The third time she phoned, Bevin said, "Hazel?"

Hazel found she couldn't hang up. Her arm was like stone and the phone was pressed hard against her ear. The silence dragged on, and she heard Bevin's soft breathing, and Hazel was afraid that she might cry. "I'm minding kids at weekends."

"I know, Sinead told me."

"Oh," Hazel said.

Before Hazel hung up, she heard her aunt say her name. The girls had tried to get her to go home for the break. Sinead had offered her house, but Hazel couldn't face the question Sinead's parents were sure to ask. She knew too that she would look for her parents and aunt. Already, whenever she woke in the house in Newcastle, she peered out her window, expecting and hoping to see her mother's parked car, though it was impossible to know what she would do if her mother was there. Her imagining didn't go beyond seeing the car and her mother's still figure. The empty street was a disappointment every time.

"Hey, is everything alright?" Sinead asked. Hazel thought she sounded nervous. It was starting to rain. Drops slid down the glass of the phone box and Hazel asked, "Did you go to my house?"

There was a muffled shout and a slamming door on the other side of the line. Hazel imagined Sinead sitting on the stairs, facing her front door, and her thick body folding inward.

"Bevin phoned the house. She wanted me to," Sinead said. "I didn't know how to tell you."

Hazel played with the cord of the phone and watched a man and his dog walk by. "She wanted to talk about you. I felt really sorry for her. She cried in the kitchen. She said she misses you, and they should have told you before now, but it wasn't her place."

"Her place? What the hell does that mean?"

Sinead said she didn't know.

"Did you see my Dad?"

Sinead took a breath. Hazel wondered if she was crying and all of a sudden she knew that Sinead had cried with Bevin. It was all Hazel could do not to hang up. "He came and stood by the kitchen door. He said hello, and asked if Bevin was alright. She said what do you think? She sounded angry."

Her mother had not appeared, and Bevin said she was in

bed. She was suffering from a sick stomach. Hazel couldn't remember her mother ever being sick enough to stay in bed, but she said nothing before hanging up.

"Bevin's so sad," Sinead said when she came back to Galway. Hazel said that she was a coward phoning Sinead and asking questions behind Hazel's back. "She knows you're a bloody softie. She didn't phone Maeve."

"I would have gone to see her too," Maeve said. They were in the kitchen cleaning up after dinner, Hazel washing and Maeve drying while Sinead made tea, a routine they'd gotten into within the first weeks of living together, with everyone taking turns.

"You said they were disgusting," Hazel said.

Maeve took the plate and shrugged. "That was the first day, the initial shock."

"What the hell are you talking about, the initial shock? So it's not as bad as you thought? After a few weeks you've gotten used to my Dad cheating on my Mom with my aunt."

"Your Mom must have forgiven them." She put her plate on the draining board. Sinead stirred the tea, and said she didn't see Hazel's mom, so they didn't know that for sure.

Hazel said, "I don't care what my mother thinks."

She got suds all over the floor and a little on Maeve's top when she flung the plate towards her.

The letter that came two weeks later did not have a stamp or address written on it, and Hazel didn't recognize the writing on the envelope, which was neater than Bevin's curving scribbles or her mother's block letters. She opened it and saw June's name on the bottom and imagined the slim woman driving from her house and walking to the door to slip the envelope through the letter box. She couldn't understand why June would travel so far, until she read the first sentences.

Hazel,

Evelyn didn't want anyone to let you know, but I've decided that it's best that you do, in case her condition worsens. Your mother was brought to Sligo hospital a few days ago. She wasn't feeling well for a while and when she went to see the doctor, he took one look at her color and rushed her into hospital. They think her body was allergic to medication she was taking and it affected her liver. After two days in Sligo, they sent her to a liver specialist in Galway. She's still there and will be for a few weeks at least. She has improved, but it was scary for a while. I thought maybe you might want to go to see her. I don't know what else to think.

June.

It was nearly 5pm. The girls were not back, and it was Hazel's turn to cook, but she didn't think of this when she grabbed her coat and ran out into the rain. Her umbrella stayed by the stairs where she'd left it minutes before, and outside raindrops ran down her face. It was cold and the streets were busy with traffic and the honk of horns. Although, Hazel hated the idea of her mother in the hospital, it was a relief to walk with a purpose. She'd started to analyze everything in the last weeks, not that she wanted to, but she might be in class or walking down the street, and she'd be hit with the memory of standing by her aunt's door. You stayed to mind me, she'd said, and her aunt had said, yes, that was part of it. She'd waited for Hazel to ask more, but she hadn't because she'd been afraid of what Bevin might say and now the photos and her mother's note haunted her. More than one night, she'd left the house when Maeve and Sinead were asleep and stood in the phone box. The coins in her hand made her hands sweat. She knew the question to ask was not, 'Will you leave?' but, 'Why did you stay?' She'd start to put the coins in the phone and would imagine her father sitting in the kitchen and reaching for the phone. So, she'd always end up leaving the phone box and walking home.

Street lights shone a yellow glow onto the ground. The hospital car park was full. She saw patients and visitors huddled outside the main door smoking and ran inside to ask where her mother was. The nurse at Admissions said Evelyn had a private room. Now that Hazel was close to her mother, she faltered. The urgency wasn't so great. At the elevators, she didn't get on, but stood back to take the letter out. Evelyn didn't want anyone to let Hazel know, but why, because Evelyn was stubborn and private, or because she was angry at Hazel for staying away? There was a lot about her mother that Hazel didn't know, but she'd thought she understood her. She was prideful and stubborn and never able to sit still, yet where was her pride when she'd learned the truth about her sister?

"Are you getting on?" The nurse was smiling at her, and Hazel stepped onto the elevator. She would not think about it. She would move towards this woman she didn't know, and try not to feel anything. Outside her mother's door, she heard voices and a soft laugh. She didn't knock, and opened the door to see her mother lying on her bed, facing away from the door. Her hand was buried in June's hair. Her mother didn't look to see who had arrived. Her gaze stayed on June, whose chair was close to the bed. Time stood still for Hazel. Nothing outside her body and those women existed. Hazel saw her mother's lingering gaze on June and then the way June shifted in her chair and looked at Hazel with a hard certainty in her eyes, and how she grabbed Evelyn's hand when Evelyn pulled away on seeing Hazel.

"Don't," June said. "It's time she knew."

Hazel stared at the women's joined hands. She couldn't look at her mother. Her mind was reeling with images of her mother smiling at the camera; her mother with June outside in the garden and coming in for breakfast in the morning. She was always out of the house by the time Hazel woke. "Some mornings I'd wake and your mother would be asleep outside."

Had she gone to June then, before Hazel was born and before Bevin arrived?

"I'm so sorry," her mother said. Hazel noticed the pasty skin and the swelling of her cheeks but it was hard to feel anything when the ground was shifting under her.

"We said we'd tell you when you were old enough, and then I didn't know how."

Hazel watched the drips slide down the bus window and thought of the figures she'd seen on the beach on her last day at home and how they'd held each other. She'd forgotten it until the hospital, or maybe she'd buried it where she'd buried her mother's long absences from her house. The affair had started those nights in the tent with June and Evelyn lying side by side and the baby asleep. Hazel's mother told her this when Hazel finally came into the room and closed the door. Now with the soothing rhythm of the bus, Hazel thought of how her mother had cried, and the silence that had weaved around the three people in the room, swelling to enhance the distance. Hazel had not gone as far as the bed. She'd leaned against the wall near the door and watched the way June looked at Evelyn and wondered how she had never noticed before.

Lorcan left for a month. He never said where he went or what he did, but he left and Evelyn cried for most of it, thinking of the way he'd paled when she told him that she'd fallen in love with someone else. He'd never guessed, not with all the mornings he'd woken alone or the nights when she left the house to walk the beach. She was scared for him and she refused to stay with June while he was gone in case he might come back to an empty house. One night, she woke to him sitting beside her on the bed crying. He had not cried before he left. He'd listened to her and had risen and gone into the shed. She'd heard banging during the night and in the morn-ing, the quiet scared her. Her foreboding didn't lessen when she realized he wasn't there. A month later, he was back and in the dim light from the hall, she saw that he'd grown painfully thin. He said he'd wanted to leave and pretend that he had never known her or this place, but he couldn't forget Hazel. Every child he saw reminded him of her and he knew the pain would only get worse. "I can't leave and I can't stay," he'd told Evelyn.

The bus stopped in the village outside Spar. A neighbor was waiting to get on. She was holding a little boy's hand and was telling him to wait. Hazel was younger than the boy when Bevin came to stay in the house. Hazel wondered how long it took for her and her father to find comfort in each other.

She didn't get a taxi. It was good to walk, though she'd slept little the night before. The girls had been annoyed when she got home. Maeve had come storming downstairs to complain about the dinner not being cooked when it was Hazel's turn, but had stopped when she saw her face.

"My mother and June," Hazel had blurted. Maeve had followed her into the kitchen and waited until Hazel fell into a chair before asking what she was talking about. Hazel had started to cry then and the force of it shocked her. In the hospital room, she'd listened to her mother and she'd felt as if the world she knew was being split open again and again.

The rain was getting heavier and her hair was stuck to her face and flat on her head. She hadn't brought a bag because she didn't know how she would feel when she saw her house. Maybe, as with her mother and June, she'd notice things she had never seen before and with it the sense of home would be lost. Or, she might feel like a woman who had been gone for too long so the place was not equal to the memories. She took the road to the left that led to the sea, and thought of walking with Bevin close to the house looking for blackberries, and cycling to the village with her father. She remembered at ten years of age, she'd fallen off the bike near the end of the road and cut her leg badly. Her father came running out of the shed when he heard her crying. He lifted her in his arms and promised that everything would be okay and she fastened her arms around his neck and clung to him.

Flight

Until a few weeks ago, Raymond wasn't concerned with John Whelan in number nine. Raymond had been keeping his eye on the McDonaghs in number eight. Mr. McDonagh had a large belly, thick graying hair and was not inclined to shave. Mrs. McDonagh was so thin that when she turned sideways, it was hard to make out what she was. The woman, who could have been anywhere from forty to fifty-five, had short brown hair and hazel eyes that changed from calm to wrath so rapidly it was unsettling.

The second week, they'd moved into the estate, she turned on Raymond when he complained that the broken down appliances in the back yard made the place look like a junkyard.

"We have a right to use our yard. We're paying rent!"

Raymond wanted to ask what kind of neighborhood allowed them to treat the place like a dump. He wanted to tell her that this wasn't one of them, but he didn't get a chance. Her eyes narrowed, and she told him it was their house and they could do what they liked. Raymond didn't bother to tell her that she was wrong. If the family failed to comply with the rules, they could get a 'Notice to Quit'. The last time he'd gone into their house, there was a hole in the kitchen door, right at the bottom, where someone, most likely Henry with his beer belly and bad temper, kicked right through.

Their kids, a girl of around twelve and a boy a little older, were trouble-makers too. The day Raymond was shooed from the door, they'd been playing ball on the road outside the houses and were making it difficult for the neighbors to drive in and out. Raymond had started taking notes on them.

He took his responsibility seriously after years of working in a factory. When his uncle first asked if he was interested in the job as rent collector and general overseer of the housing estate, Raymond almost said no. He didn't think he had the guts to go to his neighbors' doors demanding money. His mouth opened, but the word got caught in the dryness of his throat. His mother, a tall woman with grey hair, a wide waist, and lines sprouting from her grey eyes, knew he was reluctant. They'd been living together since he was born, except for ten months when he moved to Dublin and hated everything about the city, including the toast and beans he'd lived on.

He was twenty-two years old that October.

"He'll do it," she'd told her brother-in-law, who, after the death of her husband, had taken over the role of father to her son, though he never seemed entirely comfortable in

Raymond's house. The uncle preferred to take his nephew out for something to eat, or have Raymond's mother and him over to his house for dinner. Mother and son would walk to the end of the estate and through the village to get to the house on Station Road. His uncle's wife was a great cook and everyone in the town knew she baked better than anyone in Ireland, but as Raymond got older, he started to wonder on the uncle's discomfort in his child-hood home. It made Raymond wonder what his uncle knew about his father and if the uneasiness had something to do with his accident at the quarry. Whenever Raymond brought it up, his uncle would tell him there was nothing to talk about.

"I don't blame him, it's been years," Raymond's friend Alby would say, if Raymond complained. Alby's father had been working at the quarry that day, and Alby would never forget the sight of his father crying.

"But how did it bloody happen?"

Alby shrugged, "The rocks were too loose."

Raymond thought that was only the half of it.

He remembered little of his dad. When his mother asked, he lied, and told her he could recall being on the man's wide shoulders and feeling the prickly stiffness of his hair, all stone and dust from the quarry. In the last few years, his mother had started to ask about his memory more often.

"Do you remember how he used to lift you up every evening after work? You'd run out to him every single day, rain or shine."

Raymond thought it was because she was losing her

grasp on her husband. The large man was slipping through the years, to leave only a ghost of an idea and she needed someone to help keep him with her. There weren't many photos of the man. Raymond sometimes looked at the wedding pictures held in a large brown album, blanketed by thick graying paper. His mother was a slimmer, less dominant version of herself. She had short hair then too and was wearing a plain white dress with short sleeves. Her smile was relaxed and her hand lay on her new husband's leg. The groom wore a navy suit. His blonde hair was to his shoulders, and his gaze was distant, focused away from the camera, but there was an ease about him that suggested he was not wondering how this union would progress, but was merely thinking of his next pint.

Raymond looked nothing like him. He had the same dark hair and thin face as his uncle. Raymond was not so skinny in the body, and his shoulders were broader, but the uncle held himself with more certainty. He had a way of entering a room as if he'd always been there, while Raymond was self-conscious.

Getting away from the town didn't help matters. When he'd moved to Dublin for a course in business, he'd felt more out of place than ever. There were days when he didn't speak to anyone. The day he'd left the city, he'd woken and lain in his bed for ten minutes listening to the traffic and his flat-mate banging presses in the kitchen. Then he'd gotten up and found his hand reaching for his duffel-bag under the bed. He hadn't known he was leaving until that moment, but he was packed and out of the apartment within twenty minutes.

Back at home, he'd grown to be a quiet young man, who liked to sit in the pub at the weekend, and listen to the banter around him. He rarely spoke unless spoken to. As his mother grew wider, he moved further within himself. He was the kind of man who was content to be on the outskirts of a conversation, and he wasn't happy when his uncle asked him to be a rent collector. In the kitchen, with his uncle's cigarette smoke wafting to the ceiling and the tea brewing in the pot, Raymond's eyes were sore from having worked a twelve hour night shift in the factory in town, and he wanted to look his mother in the eye and say, "No, I won't take the job."

But all he managed to do was sigh and shift in his seat. When his uncle nodded at him, he shrugged, "Sure, I'll do it." Then with his uncle's prolonged stare, "Thanks, Dick."

On his first day, Raymond was surprised to discover the job wasn't as bad as he thought it would be. Unlike the factory, or the building sites he'd worked in, he felt there was a reason he had been chosen for this duty, and it wasn't because he was the nephew of the local councilor, who had taken pity on his dead end occupation. It was because Dick had seen something in Raymond that he hadn't realized until the first tenant answered the door, and Raymond became armored with cold indifference.

Raymond learned quickly. Within the first few weeks, it was hard to believe his knock used to send a shadow flitting across a window in number fifteen and an unanswered door. He had felt like an awful eejit standing with the rent book in his hand, knowing there was a Conlon inside, and there was nothing he could do. More than anything he'd felt angry, and the extent of his anger had surprised him.

When he explained the situation to Dick, he was told, "You've got to show them who's boss. You're the one who is in charge, remember that. Don't leave till they come out—knock on the window, if you have to. Let them know you've seen them, and you're not stupid."

The following week, he knocked as usual, but this time he shouted, "I know you're in there, Mr. Conlon, and I am not going anywhere until you answer your door to me. You can't expect to get away with this."

He banged on the downstairs window, before moving around to the narrow path on the side of the house and opening the back gate. The back door was unlocked and he stepped into the kitchen where he was met with Mr. Conlon's frightened face.

"I don't have any money on me."

"You'd better give me something; this is the third week. I'll have to file a report."

The man looked at Raymond, as if he couldn't place him, which wasn't surprising since Raymond could hardly recognize himself. He soon got into the habit of stepping inside each house and walking as far as the kitchen at the back. In that way, he could get a good look at how the people treated their place. If he saw something he didn't like, such as, a crack in the wall, or a broken banister on the stairs, he'd stop and look at it long enough for the resident to know something should be done. He hadn't been able to get into the McDonagh's since he stopped and stared at their kitchen door and that skinny woman blocked his path and thrust the rent money in his hand. And he noticed Mrs. Bowen from number thirty, who was newly widowed, had started to have her daughter present every Friday, as if his attention made her nervous.

But those people didn't concern him now. He was too worried about the covered boxes he'd seen John Whelan bring into his house and the weird banging noises he'd heard from upstairs when he'd arrived early to collect the rent. John's wife, tall and pretty with clear skin, fair hair and light blue eyes, looked anxious when she'd opened the front door to him. The young boy by her side had started to say something about his daddy, and the woman silenced him with a nudge.

"Is there anything I should know?" Raymond had asked her.

She'd said no. Her smile was thin.

"You know that no altering of the house can go on without permission, don't you?"

Her smile faded and she'd nodded and said she knew. He'd noticed she'd kept a firm hand on her son's shoulder.

Raymond told Dick, "I think they're up to something in nine. I saw them bringing in covered boxes from the car, and I've heard a lot of banging and shuffling upstairs. There was also a strange buzzing sound that I can't for the life of me make out."

Dick laughed, "This job suits you. Your dad would've been proud. He didn't like any messing either."

The laugh that rang between them, the male camaraderie

and the idea that Dick owed him more than he owed his long dead brother made him ask, "How did it happen, Dick? I mean, if he was so careful?"

"You know how it happened. He brought the digger too close to the edge."

Months ago, Raymond would have backed down, but now he kept his gaze fixed on Dick. "Was he drinking?"

"What are you talking about?"

"I hear things," Raymond said.

"Don't believe anything you hear in this town, especially when you've heard it in the shagging pub."

With Raymond's frustrated muteness, Dick shrugged. "You can inspect the property, if you've got any doubts. He's obviously up to something."

Dick looked at him for a while before downing the last of his cold tea and standing up from the kitchen table. "Let me know."

Raymond stayed at the table. He felt like the kitchen had suddenly grown smaller. The evening light was dull, and blocked by the net curtain, so only the strongest, thinnest streams made it through to the other side, to die on the tiled floor. He hadn't noticed how dark the room had gotten, until Dick was walking out and his thin frame was half-hidden in his slouch.

Raymond listened to the distinct retreating steps, and thought the tenants were the same as his family. They probably thought they were being coy—Mrs. Whelan and her smile, and John skipping quickly into the house with the covered boxes and getting the truck to come late in the evening. They thought they could hide things, like his mother thought she could conceal the truth about his father by making Raymond repeat a single made-up memory of running to his father in the evening. When in reality, his father was probably in the pub, and he'd been stupid enough to go to work drunk. How else could such carelessness be explained?

The next day, Raymond drove to John's place and parked out of sight. Within a half hour, he saw the wife come out with two sobbing boys. The older boy kept reaching backwards as if he wanted to run into the house, but his mother pulled him to the car. The younger son cried and was held meekly in her grasp. She looked hassled more than angry, as if she was late for an appointment and noticed nothing around her, including Raymond's green Honda Civic.

When Raymond walked up to the house five minutes later, there was no sign of life downstairs. The living room curtains were open to reveal a tidy room with a beige couch and two armchairs, facing the television which stood in the left back corner. Photos hung on the wall. He couldn't see the faces, but saw a white dress and a dark suit in one. In another, a baby and a toddler sat on the mother's and father's knees. The images didn't soften him to the man inside. He knocked on the door. There was no answer and he knocked again before deciding to walk down the side of the house. At the back, he met a locked kitchen door. He banged on the door with his fist and stepped back to see movement in the rear bedroom. There were small shadows and John's larger body in quick succession. The strangeness made Raymond feel lighter, as if the darting movements were pulling at his guts. For the first time, he was worried about what he might find, but it only made him more resolute.

"John!"

The large shadow behind the curtains stilled.

"You better let me in. I need to see what you're doing!"

"I'm sure you do," Mrs. McDonagh said, from across the brick wall. She was standing on the back steps of her house smoking a cigarette, and Raymond had to move quickly from the satisfaction in her eyes.

At the front door, he rang the doorbell, stood for a few seconds and tried again, leaving his finger on the buzzer for longer. He saw a form on the top landing and watched John come slowly down the stairs. On approach, his body was distorted by the thick front door glass. When John opened the door, Raymond noticed there were tiny cuts on his hand. "What the hell…?" he said and John shook his head stupidly. He was red in the face and sweaty.

"What are you doing in there?" Raymond demanded.

"Nothing," John answered.

"I have to see." He was willing to push through, but he didn't have to. John stepped out of the way. "I can explain if you let me."

Raymond looked at him long and hard, but when no explanation came, just an alert weariness from his eyes; he started for the stairs. John was quick after him.

"Wait, J.P. got in and opened them…."

Raymond was taking the stairs two at a time, and ignored the plea. Outside the bedroom door, John gripped his arm and Raymond pushed him off and sent him back against the wall. His blue eyes narrowed on John. Raymond's father had had the same eyes, a warm sky-blue, but there was nothing warm in the son's gaze before the door opened. He saw the opened cages, and the sound of fluttering wings reached inside him. The bright yellow and brilliant greens of the birds made Raymond gape with wide eyes, but it was their timid smallness as they rode towards the ceiling that made his body tingle with a memory of being held in rough hands. Raymond had a sudden urge to cry, and he watched one yellow budgie weave towards him and seek escape with eyes full of hope before John jumped between them and closed the door.

THE CLOWN PRINCE

HIS DAUGHTER USED TO SIT BESIDE HIM when he put on make-up. It had been hard not to grab her hand when she reached for his face. If she smeared his make-up, he didn't shout because he didn't want to scare her. Now he wondered if he should have been a little sinister. Maybe, she would have remained interested if she'd lingered at the bedroom door, awed with the sight of him, or if his wife pulled her away and said, "No, leave Daddy alone."

"But it's not Daddy," his daughter might have said.

With the make-up, his name changed to Jean, after Jean Gerard Debaru, but his daughter kept calling him Daddy. Eventually, she'd gotten bored with his silence and routine until the boredom changed to something worse, which he tried not to think about. But it was hard when he heard his wife and daughter mumbling in the kitchen. There was an undercurrent of irritation in their low voices. He heard every movement because he was motionless at the dresser. His foundation was done and he was about to outline his mouth and eyes. Once he started doing that, their voices would blend into the background, and his reflection would become the most important thing. He had to concentrate so the lines around his eyebrows didn't flow downwards and give him a mean look.

Twenty minutes later, he heard the run of water and knew the kettle was being put on. No-one asked if he wanted tea because that meant walking down the hall to the bedroom. For the last couple of weeks, they'd stayed away while he was getting ready.

His shoulder-length hair was pulled back by a hairband. He was going grey. His daughter was starting college.

"What will I tell people?" she'd said, and it had nearly broken his heart, but he'd smiled and said, "You can tell them that laughter is the shortest distance between two people."

"Said the clown prince of Denmark." His wife had spoken in her off-hand way that wasn't off-hand at all.

His daughter groaned, "Please tell me there isn't a clown prince."

"Of course there is, your daddy."

His daughter gave a little screech before storming out of the kitchen.

"You did say Denmark," he'd said, "When have I ever been to Denmark?"

If laughter was the shortest distance between two people, he wondered what was the longest—a lack of?

He wore surgical gloves, and the soft and malleable material was strange on his hands. Still, they helped him forget his age because his hands showed the years the most. The skin had gotten loose, but that was not why he wore the gloves. He'd only started wearing them after he went to the International Clown Festival in Ballygaddy.

"Do you realize for some people that would be a nightmare?" his daughter said when he told her about it. "Could you imagine Liz there? She'd shit herself."

"Watch your mouth."

"Sorry Mom, but she really would. I'm not afraid of clowns, but I think I would too. There's got to be something else there. They can't have a festival with thousands of clowns. It's insane."

"No, that's all there is, millions of us." He'd loved his daughter's wide-eyed stare that never stayed long.

His wife laughed. "Don't listen to him. There'll be jugglers and street performers and puppeteers. They're what I'm going for."

He'd felt the dart of his daughter's gaze. It had been years since they'd watched him perform.

As it happened, his wife didn't go because her mother fell and suffered concussion and her father called to tell her to come home at once.

"Aren't you done?"

His wife was leaning against the doorframe with a mug in her hands. She was a small fair-haired woman with soft features. Yellow light from the hall spread around her and made her body look limp and tired.

"Je rêvasse."

He didn't know why he slipped into French so much now. Usually, he uttered single words that made his wife straighten, but now she nodded and said, "Daydreaming again." He realized he'd said this frequently in the last few months. In front of his mirror, he liked to pretend he was in one of the mirrored classrooms of École de Mimodrame in Paris, or in one of the many student apartments he'd frequented, or the Geary Theatre where he was asked to appear. But all those places led back to the dark room with the curtains half-closed, the unmade bed and his make-up on the dresser, which had been moved from the bathroom two weeks ago because he took too much time, and they only had one bathroom.

"Dad, come on," his daughter had insisted from the bathroom door.

"Don't call me Dad." He'd said angrily. His daughter was taken aback. It was surprising how fast the tears came. She didn't even blink. She was still standing there when he turned back to the mirror. He'd felt the strain come from her like a vibration.

"What should she bloody call you?" his wife said later. It was dark outside. His feet were sore and his stomach ached where the boy had run into him head-first. He'd wanted to say with make-up on, he was Jean. He'd wanted to say that he was not a clown but an artist, but all hed said was, "I was getting ready and in the zone."

"What the fuck? In the zone? You scared her."

"Ha." It was more a burst of breath than a laugh, and his wife had stared at him for a few seconds before rising from the kitchen table and leaving him alone.

"You look tired," his wife said now and he sat straighter.

"I'm fine."

"You hate birthday parties."

"They're alright."

She gave a slight chuckle, and he refused to let his defenses down. "Last week, you said there must be birthday parties in hell."

Last week, the child screamed when she saw him.

"We must suffer for our art," he said.

"Must we make others suffer?"

He wanted her to go, but she was shuffling into the room, that's what he would call it. She sat on the bed.

"They're going to close applications soon."

He refused to say anything, and moved his face closer to the mirror. He had a long face, but not thin so he looked substantial. It was a face hard to miss: a lengthy nose, wide eyes, full lips, thick hair. He could make out the side of her face: a turned up chin, a stream of blonde hair.

"You know Jane is going to college." Her voice had risen in the way it did when she got impatient or upset.

The tone got inside his skin. If she did it again, his hand would shake.

"Not now," he said.

"Then when? You'll be tired and angry later. Sunday you'll be on the street."

On the street, she knew where he was going. Why not legitimize it with a name? Did she really think of him on the street, like a beggar? Well, he'd prefer to beg than stand before twenty-odd bored children spouting French.

"It's getting tough. Even if you had parties every weekend, we'd hardly make it."

They'd been doing alright before the Celtic Tiger went scurrying into a corner to die and left the country in recession. He'd held frequent workshops and taught in schools, but his wife had forgotten that. She acted as if he had no chance of building the business up again.

"Are you wearing gloves?"

He'd forgotten about the gloves and fought the urge to hide them or yank them off. That would only make her curious, and she'd ask what was wrong and why he never talked to her anymore. He was not in the mood for one of those conversations, so he said, "Yes, I'm wearing gloves."

Denise had given him a pair. Or rather, she'd hidden a pair in his bag. He'd been shocked when he found them while unpacking. It was Monday morning, and his wife was in the shower, but it could have been Sunday night when he took them out, and his wife could have been with him, or she could have unpacked herself. Denise might have imagined his wife as the type to do his laundry, which she was, but he was not the type to let her. He would not chance missing socks on anyone.

The gloves had smelled of cinnamon and before he knew it, he was putting them on. The excitement was such that Denise might as well have been on the bed in front of him. He imagined her large breasts, the soft pillow of her belly, the wild bush of pubic hair, and he'd kept the gloves on until he heard his wife's steps.

He leaned towards the mirror and pretended to fix a mouth that was already set and powdered, while his wife's question why hung between them. Finally, he said, "I don't like the feel of make-up on my skin."

"Since when?"

Since he'd stopped by Denise's open hotel door and was caught by the mass of her dark hair and the strange perverseness of her gloved hands dipping into the white make-up.

"Since forever, I just never said."

His wife stared at him.

"You won't need to put on any more make-up. You'll have weekends and summers off. We could go places and do things together for once, Alexander."

"Please, I need to get ready," he said.

"The only road to strength is through vulnerability," he'd said, when he was standing behind Denise. He didn't say he'd stolen the line from Stephan Nachmonovitch. Nor did he think of the first time he'd said this to his wife when she'd cried about her family's strict Presbyterian rules and her fear of her father.

His hands moved down Denise's arms and upward to her shoulder. She quivered and gripped his wrists. They stayed still for a long time watching each other in the mirror; the woman with her white painted face and the man free of make-up, until she stood and without a word closed the door.

He performed naked in her room with his face painted. His movements were slow and guarded. She told him she felt uncouth beside him. Her gestures were vulgar and obscene compared to his, and he said he was just a clown. She asked if Pierrot was just a clown and he laughed, and said, of course not. Pierrot was the tragic avatar struggling to find a place in the bourgeois world. She asked if he was struggling. He said, isn't everyone, and lay beside her mound of soft flesh, so warm and sweet.

For the next two days, they hardly left the room. He painted his face and mimed routines he'd forgotten about for years. She refused to perform each time he asked. She said she would probably give up now that she'd seen him. Late into their second day, he asked if she felt pity when she watched him. He saw the confusion in her eyes, before she said, "Maybe a little."

She said, "It's hard to know exactly what I'm feeling, but there's definitely something like that."

So he relayed to her the story of his wife.

He said after knowing his wife a few weeks, he asked her to meet him on Grafton Street. It was the middle of summer and a bright day. The city was full of people. He put on his white outfit and his white make-up, and got there an hour before his wife was due. By the time she arrived, a crowd had gathered. He was on his unicycle when he saw her stroll towards him. He paused, so Denise nudged him and said, "Okay, go on".

He said he had a rose.

"Did you hold it for the whole performance?" Denise wanted to know. He waved her question away. It hardly mattered. What was important was the look on his wife's face when he emerged from the crowd, splitting bodies to land at her feet. He bowed and handed her the rose. The crowd cheered. His wife went red and looked left and right, as if seeking escape. He thought she would not take it, but she did. He didn't say anything, but when she looked at him, he was sure she knew him. He'd always been a big man, an imposing figure. She lingered to watch him, but when he finished and looked for her, she was gone.

The hotel was a beehive of laughter and footsteps. Their bodies were sinking into the middle of the bed. He told Denise of his thrill when he saw the rose had been placed in a chipped mug in his wife's student accommodation. His wife told him she'd been shocked to see the clown coming to her. She said it was peculiar, but sweet. She stayed to watch him, and he was really very good. For his size, he had such grace of movement.

He was excited and emboldened. He grasped her hands, but when he was about to tell her that he was the clown, she sighed in a way that stopped him from speaking and said there was something sad and needy in the way he kept glancing at her. It made her uncomfortable. She said she couldn't help feeling sorry for him.

Alexander finished, and Denise's silence stunned him. He'd expected disdain and disbelief; for her to ask what was wrong with his wife. How could she not see the difference between the performance and the performer? He'd expected Denise to understand that his wife's sorrow had nothing to do with him, at least not in the way she saw it. The sorrow may have come from the place he'd reached, but it was entirely hers.

Denise asked, "What did you do?"

A peal of laughter came from the room upstairs. It sounded as if someone was running on the spot. Alexander's grandiose body allowed no slipping away, his mood no gradual disentanglement. He pushed Denise off, and her upper body flopped onto the bed. She might have been surprised, maybe a little wounded, but he refused to look. He pulled his sweatpants on and said he was hungry. The restaurants were packed so they bought bread, cheese and luncheon meat from the supermarket and a bottle of whiskey for Alexander, for Denise a bottle of gin. These forays for food and drink were the only times they saw the festivities. Until the final day, his phone stayed in his room two doors down. Denise would don a t-shirt and stand in the hall any time her mobile rang. Her bathroom was too quiet she said. At least there was one advantage to the people running around at all hours. He didn't think of checking his phone until the day he was leaving, and when he did, he'd felt like he'd swallowed a rock. He imagined his wife had called ten, twelve, thirteen times, 'where are you, please call, we're so worried,' but she'd called only twice, and left a message to say she hoped he was having fun, and things were strained as usual.

He told himself that Denise didn't want to hear of his wife, just as he didn't want to hear of her shy husband, and that kept him from finishing the story, though the threads of it hung between them. His wife remained in the room with them, with her whisper. "I felt sorry for him."

Years ago, it had made him angry. "Do you feel sorry for me?" he'd said. He saw his wife's confusion, and a blast of something else in her eyes that he refused to dwell on. She'd said, "No, of course not."

"Well I feel sorry for you," he'd said, and he'd said some cruel things about the simplicity of her thought; how it was easy to see how her father could control her, a little puppet with no ideas of her own and no tools to see the realities of the world and the beauty that lay beyond it. She'd been shocked into silence.

So many years after the fact, the memory made him sullen, because no matter what he said, his wife never forgot the pity she'd felt. It had clung to her, and knowledge of it meant the ease he and Denise enjoyed their first night and day, when they were able to watch each other through the mirror or lie entangled on the bed without need of distraction, could not be resurrected—so they drank too much. Of Saturday night, Alexander remembered little. A fumble under the covers that ended up with one of them on the floor, or maybe both, he couldn't be sure, and a quick dart to the bathroom to get sick. They were hungover when they said goodbye. He didn't know if he should kiss her and decided by her stiff smile it was best not to. He stepped out of her room and thought when she closed the door that maybe he should have left before then. But he decided not to dwell on that final goodbye or Denise's discomfort when he returned form the bathroom seconds before he left her. He knew she'd taken the opportunity to put the gloves into his bag then.

He didn't say goodbye to his wife and daughter before leaving for the birthday party. The address took him to a well-to-do area. Steep steps led to the front door. The windows, of which there were eight, were tall. It was a large house; 'looming' was the word he would use. The squeals of children reached him when he got out of the car.

His daughter's childhood birthday celebrations had taken place in Sligo, a small village by the sea, with her cousins, two boys and a girl from the older sister, and two girls from the younger, a stepladder of ages with Jane in the middle. There'd been dinner and cake, but no mention of entertainment, certainly not of Alexander supplying it, though he'd often be asked by the other villagers.

"Bonjour," he said to the slender woman walking towards him now. After twenty years, his English was perfect and had sprinkles of Dub in it, but French had an effect on women. They were less inclined to judge

"Jean?" she asked, as if some other white-faced man might have gone to her house without an appointment.

"Oui," he said.

Her hand was soft and her fingers so long he could feel them wrap around him like snakes. She smiled. There was the fleeting look over his face where signs of age protruded like cracks on paint. His hair was pulled back, but there was a patch of grey at the front that he could do nothing about. The woman disengaged herself. She had grave eyes and a haughty chin. "I thought you'd be younger," she said with no hint of embarrassment. Rather, she seemed accusatory. He shrugged, and thought he should feel angry, but he couldn't be bothered.

"Those photos were taken when I first came here," he said, "It's hard to take them down."

"Oh," she said, "Do you still do workshops?"

Was there a hint of humor in her tone? She'd spoken softly, but without effort. Her head tilted a little as if she'd caught him in a lie.

"Mostly during the summer," he said.

She smiled and asked him to follow her. He reminded her that he needed to set up and she told him that could wait for a minute. It was not unusual for the hosts to want to show him the area before he took everything out of the car so he wasn't surprised, though he expected her to bring him around the back garden instead of towards the front steps. His forty-five minutes must have started by now or at least were close to starting. As if she'd read his thoughts, she told him that the children started a game of Rounder's, or rather, her husband and brother-in-law started a half hour ago. It was in full swing, and she was loath to finish it too soon. If he wouldn't mind waiting inside just for a bit, they'd pay him for his time. He could add another forty-five minutes onto their bill, though she assured him that it wouldn't take that long,

She paused at the front door and he was thinking 'loath', he was thinking 'or rather' and wanted to shove her forty minutes up her arse, but he needed the money, and he had no more appointments. He said he had a party after this so, he could wait twenty minutes tops.

"Great."

The house echoed. There was a smell of lemon. The hall was wide and the ceiling so high he couldn't resist looking up. The floor was black and white tiles, and the curving staircase sparkled. He spied a kitchen opposite the front door with an Island messy with dishes. A window with a view of the garden took up the back wall. He saw the green leaves of trees but they were too high to see the action. She led him to the right and opened a solid wooden door. With one step inside the room, she paused and seemed taken aback. "I didn't know you were here."

There was no answer, and he imagined a drunken relative sprawled on the couch or a stern mother-in-law watching the game with arms crossed. He took the woman's glance and smile as an apology, so he was surprised to see a young girl of around ten by the window. She'd pulled a stool to the sill and her chin was resting on her hand. Her gaze was caught on the game outside, though she was sitting with a stiffness that told him she was not seeing what was going on. She was dressed in jeans and a black sweater, which didn't fit with the elegance of the surroundings. There was little space in the room, but it was not small, as much as crowded, with footstools, little corner tables, magazine racks, a coffee table and armchairs, and a couch in the middle of it all. He had to step gently to the fireplace where a fire was burning low. The carpet and three piece suite was white.

He declined her offer of a drink or a snack.

"I won't keep you waiting long," the woman said. She didn't introduce him to the girl, nor did she glance at the girl or say anything to her before leaving them alone.

The second the door shut, the girl looked at him and he saw she'd been crying. Her eyes were red, and her nose was running slightly. He smiled, and waved with a gloved hand. He thought of the woman's long fingers and looked to the girls hand on the sill for resemblance. There was none in the face. The girl had a rounder face and eyes that were wide apart. Her hair was brown instead of black like the woman's. A yell from outside followed by another shout caught the girl's attention. It could have been some accident; a child out there was probably crying, but the girl's expression had not changed. He thought he'd never seen anything sadder. She was cocooned in her sorrow. He wondered what her story was. A child from a first marriage perhaps, a child unloved by the stepmother and forced to watch instead of being allowed participate. Or maybe, her sorrow was a constant heavy burden that the mother couldn't cope with anymore. "If you must be miserable, be miserable inside."

He cleared his throat. She looked at him again, and this time he bowed. Her face showed no curiosity when he was upright again. There was little place for his large body. He had an urge to fall over, to drip over the footstool, to flounder across the table, but her seriousness kept that urge back as did the fear of embarrassment if she continued to look at him without a trace of humor.

He brought one arm up towards his head. The hand was flat as if he was holding a tray. He smiled and lifted his legs high. He walked on the spot and looked like he was treading water. He was the waiter holding the plate high in his hands. His body went this way and that as if in avoidance of obstacles. He looked towards his left, became still and smiled. He'd found his table. He put the plate gently down and moved to the unseen table and bent his knees. He was sitting with his invisible knife and fork, and grimaced as he tried to cut the food. He frowned and looked at the girl. She could have been a painting. He pretended to attack his food with a sledge and hammer. He jumped back alarmed and looked all around him as the plate went flying and he was pulled by an invisible hand. He fell forward and stumbled downward as if he is falling through the sky and there was no floor under his feet. Once landed and steady, he felt his head to make sure he was all in one piece. He looked around him before he opened an imaginary curtain and peered through.

He lost the girl. There was cheering outside, and she turned away from him. He was breathless and hot, and it took a while for his heart to settle. His mouth was dry, but it was hardly important when all he wanted was to see the girl smile. The clock above the mantle ticked loudly, and he thought of his daughter staring out the kitchen window when he was leaving. He wondered if she was still there, and if she would look at him when he came back. Another cheer, and he decided he'd wait only a few more moments for the girl to glance at him.

WALKING A COUNTRY ROAD

LEANNE COULDN'T REMEMBER HER MOTHER ever going into her father's house. She'd scoffed at the place when he'd first moved in. She'd called it depressing and drab. She said it suited her ex-husband perfectly, right down to the cracking stone wall and the rusty gate. She said it was typical that he'd get a place so close to his mother and looking right onto the road where everything had happened because he wanted to suffer. Leanne told her mother to shut up then, because Leanne didn't like hearing the word 'suffer'. It made her think of Mass with her gran and Christ on the cross, and she didn't want to think of her father in those terms.

Her mother said, "It's true. He's got one foot in her grave."

Then she sighed and said, 'He wasn't always like that."

When her parents first separated, her mother said that their move back to Sligo changed her father. She said they should have stayed in London. But then, not long ago she said it was Leanne who changed him because he'd started to think of his sister as a little girl and of her being as vulnerable as Leanne and it killed him.

"I think what happened to his sister never really hit him until he held you. Do you remember he wouldn't let you anywhere, not even out the back garden without someone trailing behind you?"

He still hardly let Leanne out of his sight, but she didn't say that because whenever Leanne said something about her father, her mother's frown and widening eyes were full of drama. And Leanne hated the way her mother probed. When her father ordered Leanne to wash the eyeshadow off, Leanne told her mother on the way home. Her mother had grown tense and swerved to park the car the first chance she got. Then she'd turned to face Leanne and asked, "What did he do?"

"I just told you what he did. He made me wash my face. God Mom, stop being so dramatic."

"If he touches you, you need to tell me."

Leanne wanted to scream.

"He didn't," she said, which was not exactly the truth.

She told Tracy that her father scared her when he pulled her towards the bathroom and shouted at her, but her mother was worse for going all crazy over it. At least her father apologized.

Leanne swore to only talk to Tracy about her visits with her father because Tracy said things like, "Poor thing." So it was actually about Leanne.

Lately, Tracy and Leanne's conversations had been about Leanne's upcoming birthday. It fell on a Saturday, and Tracy was trying to encourage her to have a party. The last time they'd spoken of it, Tracy said that Leanne could stay with her dad on Friday or the Sunday night of that weekend. "You only turn thirteen once. He's got to understand."

They were lying on Tracy's bed. The room smelled of air freshener, which barely masked the smell of cigarette smoke. Tracy's brother had just stopped banging on the door, demanding entry and with a softer hushed voice a cigarette. Tracy had told him to get lost. "They're saying he has A.D.H.D now", Tracy said when he left, "which means, Asshole, Dickhead, Hello did I say Dickhead?"

Leanne laughed. Tracy nudged her and said, "So will you ask him."

Leanne said, "Yeah maybe."

"Are you scared?"

"Don't be stupid," Leanne said.

When Leanne's mother turned off her engine outside the father's house and got out of her car, Leanne knew Tracy's mother must have said something to her about the upcoming birthday.

"What are you doing?" Leanne said, over the car roof. It was drizzly and cold, and Leanne was in a bad mood already. She hadn't wanted to come out here. Up until a year ago, she wouldn't have dreamed of not seeing her dad and gran, but she was getting tired of driving the five miles to the country every weekend. Her mother said she needed to talk to her dad about her birthday.

"It's a bad birthday for your dad," her mother said.

"What did Mrs. Lowry say?" Leanne asked.

"You know she disappeared at thirteen."

"She didn't disappear," Leanne said.

"Okay," her mother said. "She was murdered at thirteen." Her mother paused and her face scared Leanne because of the new softness in the eyes that came before bad news. "You know it was her thirteenth birthday."

Leanne felt sick. It was as if her aunt's ghost had touched her. There was a feel of clammy warmth on her skin. "So?" she said, but the urge to cry was in her voice. All her life, she'd felt her aunt's shadow on her and now this.

"So, I want you to stay in town with me. I don't want you coming here."

A car went by, and there was a beep of the horn. Someone they knew, probably a friend of the grans, though neither thought to wave.

"You shouldn't have told me," Leanne said. Her gran had told her many things in secret, but not that it was her aunt's birthday. This reinforced the idea of her mother's cruelty.

"They would have," her mother said. The wind blew the branches of the trees across the road and her mother's hair across her face. She held the strands back.

"No, they wouldn't have."

"Do you not want me to ask him?"

Leanne heard the door open behind her. She closed her eyes, a blink, where she imagined being in Tracy's bedroom.

"Are you coming in?" her father shouted.

Her mother gave up on her hair. She said, "Leanne?"

Leanne started for the door without answering. She wanted to stay in town and have a party for once. She hated the thought of having to come out here to have dinner and cake with her dad and gran. She was never able to go on her phone without her dad glaring in a way that made her uncomfortable, so she'd put it away and then he'd say "Good girl," as if she had a choice.

But on the other hand, the thought of her mother and father in the same room made her nervous, so she said nothing and didn't know how to feel when she heard the click clack of her mother's steps behind her.

"Hi Dad," Leanne said. He nodded in answer before he stepped back to let her into the 'cottage' as he called it. There was a fire going in the living room and an underlying smell of grease. The room was lit by a lamp in the far corner and another by the door. There wasn't much sunlight, due to the smaller windows set into the wall. Before the end of the day, she'd have gotten used to it.

Her mother was standing in the doorway. Her face was hard to make out with the dull day on her back. She had extensive cheeks and seemed breathless from the short walk to the house.

"Can I come in?" she asked. Leanne hated how nervous her mother sounded and the way she seemed to retreat into herself.

Her father shrugged and said sure. Her mother stepped inside, but didn't close the door. She asked how her father was and he said, "What is it Grace?"

Her mother glanced at Leanne, who was looking at her feet. Cold air came through the front door. In the distance, Leanne thought she could hear a seagull cawing on its way to the sea.

"Leanne wants to have a party with her friends on her birthday. She can come out here Friday or Sunday if that's better for you. I don't mind coming out early Monday morning to take her to school."

Leanne's father glanced at her. It was hard to get used to the gloom of the house, but he was getting clearer and his face looked stark and hurt.

"Is that what you want?"

She shrugged.

Her mother said, "Leanne?"

Her father told her mother to stop. "She had a tongue last time I saw her."

He was looking at Leanne now, "Speak up! What do you want?"

"I don't mind," Leanne said. She couldn't look at her mother for fear she might cry.

"Right. So it's settled." There was a flap of hope in Leanne's chest before he said, "You'll have her until 5p.m, and then I can celebrate with her. That's how we've been doing it for the last five years."

Her mother said, "Please," and Leanne felt she was shriveling up. When her mother said "Please," and her father said, "Don't, Grace," Leanne disappeared from them. She was a shadow in the room, an afterthought that would reappear once the shouts were finished and the doors slammed.

Her mother said her father wouldn't know how to celebrate. He was incapable of enjoying anything, because he was so caught up in the past and his guilt. The idea of his guilt startled Leanne and made her look at her father. She could study him now that she was invisible, and he was bearing up to her mother. She saw a drop in his jaw and a tightness to his features that might have been vulnerability, only Leanne thought it was surprise, and a little bit of hatred. She knew her mother's comment had to do with her aunt because everything did. She waited for her father to say, "Fuck you" or "You're some bitch", but he said nothing. He stood still, while her mother pushed her hair from her face.

The room they'd stood in was basic, a couch, an armchair and a television. Outside a truck rumbled by and a dog barked in the farm next door. "Are you finished?" her father finally said.

And her mother made a sound like a yelp. "Why can't you think of her for once?"

"If this was about her, you would have phoned or you could have come out by yourself."

"What is that supposed to mean?"

Leanne's hands were in her coat pocket; one gripped her phone. She thought of Tracy, and it helped to keep the bad feelings down. Sometimes, she didn't know what she felt when things like this happened. The emotion was a disorienting feeling that made her stomach turn. It was not exactly sorrow because, although she wanted to cry, she wanted to stamp her feet and scream too. Her mother's voice had risen. She said he never answered his phone when she tried to call. He always made things difficult. Her father said her mother always wanted things her way, and she didn't care about anyone else. She just wanted Leanne's gran to suffer, by keeping Leanne away on her birthday. And her mother said, "What's the difference in waiting one more week for the bloody cake?"

Her father said, "Why can't she wait one more week for the party, like she always does? Are her friends more important than her gran and father? Is that what you're getting at?"

And her mother made the mistake of bringing up the number thirteen again, which threw her father into a temper and he said, "You're the one making a big fucking deal of it."

Her mother said, "But it is a big deal, isn't it?"

The silence cracked with antagonism. Leanne's body felt tired. Every word they'd spoken was a weight on her.

"I'm sorry Leanne," her mother said. Leanne still felt invisible, yet her mother had managed to pull her into the fight; it was like being grabbed by her hair.

"Leanne doesn't need your sympathy," her father said.

"No, you're the one who needs sympathy, but I can't give you any more."

"Okay," her father said, while the rise in tone said that it was not okay at all. He never scared Leanne but sometimes she felt unsure around him. She wouldn't have been surprised if he lunged forward and pushed her mother out the door, though she couldn't remember witnessing any kind of violence with him.

"Is that it?" her father said.

Her mother sighed and said, "I'm sorry," only this time Leanne didn't know who she was saying it too.

Leanne was named after her aunt and she hated the way the name hung on her. She thought as soon as she could she would change her name legally. She would become Alison, or Mary, or Jane. She would choose names that could be overlooked. But mostly she would choose a name that didn't hurt her father whenever he uttered it and didn't make her grandmother sigh. She would be herself and not a body with someone else's face because that was how she felt. Every time they said Leanne, they saw a ghost.

Leanne and her aunt didn't look alike. At least it didn't seem so from the photos. Her gran said they had the same eyes, which Leanne hated hearing because she imagined her eyes on a dead girl. It was the shape her gran was talking about. Both had big eyes, rabbit eyes, Tracy called them, though she knew Leanne hated that.

Leanne had her father's height, her mother's blue eyes, and thick mousy-colored hair that she grew long, and Tracy's mother trimmed when needed.

Leanne's aunt's eyes had been brown like her father's. The aunt had had a thin face like him too, which was encased with curly hair that was long the last time her image had been captured before the tragedy, as her gran called it, though Leanne thought tragedy was the wrong word. The right way to describe it was ugliness.

The first time she remembered her father saying the world was an ugly place, she was eight. She wanted to walk to her gran's house alone. The road was winding and shaded by the Coolaney Mountains and watched by cows. There were instances of traffic, but there was a footpath on the opposite side of the road to her father's and gran's houses.

Leanne's idea was to phone her gran and get her to wait outside. Leanne had often walked to Tracy's house while the mothers kept watch from their gardens. They only lived three doors down from each other. You could just make out the roof of her gran's house from her father's back garden and the thought of walking alone out there was exhilarating. Leanne had imagined telling Tracy, but her father brought her to the window of his house and pointed out at the road, and said that was where his sister went before she disappeared.

"She wasn't going far either," he said.

When Leanne told her mother later, she said, "Jesus Christ, he makes a walk sound morbid."

Leanne asked what morbid meant and her mother glanced at her and said he wasn't always like that. She was driving and her face had puckered in the way it used to, when she thought of her ex-husband. Leanne didn't persist, though she felt like screaming with her mother's refusal to explain morbid. Being around the adults was like stepping over holes.

There was so much missing and so many things left to guess-work it was hard to think.

The gran's house was a compact bungalow set from the road with a view of the mountains and the river gushing behind it. When her mother collected Leanne from there, she'd give one blast of the horn and wait outside. Leanne's gran went to the window each time to peer out, "Too good for us now," she'd say.

Eventually Leanne said, "Gran thinks you're snobby because you never come in."

Her mother said, "Her house is too bloody depressing. It's a mausoleum to the dead."

Leanne asked what a mausoleum was and her mother said, "She knows it makes him suffer."

Mausoleum-
NOUN
1. A building, especially a large and stately one, housing
   a tomb or tombs.
This definition led Leanne to look up tomb.

Tomb-
NOUN
1. A large vault, typically an underground one, for bury
   ing the dead.

Leanne said her gran's house was not a mausoleum, because her aunt was buried in the graveyard in Colloony.

Her mother said, "What about all those photos?"

Leanne shrugged. As she got older, she started to notice the way her father's shoulders caved in the moment he was on his mother's driveway, and she'd realize it was because of the photos. It reminded Leanne of the competitions she and Tracy used to have to see who could stay under water the longest. Leanne had a sense that Tracy disappeared whenever she'd become fully submerged, though Leanne could see her. It was like that with her father in her gran's house, a sense that he'd gone somewhere else though he was right there.

One particular photo seemed to get to him more than any other and it was on her gran's dresser in the living room. He never looked at it.

The photo showed her aunt and father sitting on the front steps of Gran's house. Her aunt had her hand up to block the sun from her eyes, and Leanne's father was leaning towards her. They were smiling broadly. Her aunt was wearing a dress. Her knees touched and her feet were positioned outwards so her legs took up the shape of a triangle with her dress pulled down. Leanne's father had a soccer ball on his knees.

Her Gran told Leanne that her father was ten, and her aunt was thirteen, and it was last picture they had of her aunt.

"One day she left and never came back. She might as well have taken your Grandfather with her, might as well have dug the grave for him then and there."

Leanne knew about the graves by then, and that her aunt

and grandfather were angels watching over her. But it would be another year before her father would lead her to the window to look at the road where her aunt had been taken.

"Where did she go?" Leanne asked her gran.

Gran held Leanne's hand and brought her to the couch and sat her down. Gran had her apron on, and there was flour on her cheeks. She smelled like bread.

She said, "Do you know the story of Little Red Riding Hood?"

Leanne said yes, and Gran told her that the wolf was real, but he didn't always come into the house. Sometimes the wolf hid outside waiting for Red Riding Hood to be alone and then it pounced.

Leanne had nightmares for weeks after this, and she was reluctant to go into her gran's house for fear the wolf had gotten inside, though she never admitted the cause of her dread to her parents. Her father and mother never wanted to talk about her aunt, and there was something about the way her gran sat after she'd spoken, with her eyes downcast and her hand holding Leanne's, that told Leanne that this was a special thing between the two of them, and if she wanted her gran to talk again, she'd have to keep quiet.

In the years to come, her gran was able to delve into the truth of the aunt and father and bring Leanne onto that step to tell her what had happened next. Alone in the house, her gran would hold the photo and say that the aunt had stood afterwards and declared that she was taking a walk. Gran told Leanne about the search. When the aunt didn't come back, they'd called every friend she had. The search lasted three days and Leanne's father went everywhere with her grandfather to look for her. None of them slept. They sat in the living room, hoping every rustle of grass was the aunt coming home. On the fourth morning, they found her. After the funeral, the grandfather was every day at the Garda Station asking what they were doing, and if they'd found the person who'd taken their girl from them. His heart finally gave out from the pain of it.

Sometimes, her gran held the photo and talked about the grandfather Leanne never knew. Other times she talked about the aunt, and her love of animals and her bright laughter. She'd say it was tough because, after all this time, she couldn't speak about the aunt to Leanne's father, without seeing the hurt. She'd squeeze Leanne's hand and say, "But I can talk to you."

And Leanne knew it was because she'd kept the wolf secret. "Do you understand?" her gran had said that day, and seven-year-old Leanne had nodded. Her gran told her she was a smart girl. "Now, do you want to see if the loaf is ready?"

Leanne had nodded again. On their way to the kitchen, Leanne glanced at the wedding photo of her mother and father that still hung on the wall. Within a few months, that photo would be taken down and eventually it would be hard for Leanne to remember her parents together.

She was in secondary school when she told Tracy about the wolf, and they looked up the story so she could fill in the gaps. Leanne typed *Girl disappears from Ballisadare,* and the date that she'd seen on her aunt's gravestone.

"Oh my God," Leanne said. She grasped Tracy's hand, "Look what happened to her."

"Are you hungry?" Leanne's father said, once the front door had closed and Leanne had wiped the tears from her eyes. Leanne said sure, though the argument had unsettled her stomach. Her father didn't mention her birthday again. He cooked chips and sausages, and afterwards they drove to the local shop for ice cream. He talked about his week in the garage, and the woman who'd gotten a loan of a car while hers was being fixed. She brought the car back with dog fur all over the front and back seats, and vomit that might have been the dogs or might not. He couldn't tell. He said there were dents on the front bonnet and half-eaten burgers in the boot.

"Gross, did you have to clean it?" Leanne asked.

He said, "Well she wasn't going to. If I see her coming again, I'll run a mile."

Leanne laughed, and for a while she forgot about the chance she'd lost, only for it to hit her with renewed force when she woke the next morning to Tracy's text. *Well what happened?*

She couldn't bring herself to answer. She was having lunch with her father when the second alert came in, and she looked at him, and he said, "You better turn it off after. You're leaving soon."

"Is everything okay?" he said, when she'd been staring at the text for several seconds. She felt as if the blood had drained to her toes. There was a sense of dizziness and for a moment, she had the sensation of being in the room with her parents again, only this was worse.

Your Mom told us what happened! Why didn't you say you wanted a party? What's wrong with you?

"Leanne?"

She turned off her phone without answering the text, though the words stayed in her head. *What's wrong with you?* It was hard to concentrate on anything else for the rest of the day, which made her father snap at her during Sunday dinner and her gran tell him to take it easy.

When her mother beeped the horn, Leanne ran out of her gran's house. She slammed the passenger door and didn't answer when her mother asked how her night was. On the road, Leanne put on the radio and turned the volume up. Her mother snapped it off and said, "Is there something wrong? What did he do?"

"*He* didn't do anything. You had to talk about me to Tracy, didn't you?"

Leanne hated that she was crying. To her right was the bay. The tide was out, and the sand was dark and muddy looking. A single boat was barely discernible; a dot of white against the grey sky. Her mother was driving slowly with her neck craned over the wheel, and Leanne thought her father would laugh if her mother came into the garage with her plastic seat coverings and the furry steering wheel.

"What was I supposed to say?" Her mother said.

"Nothing, okay! You were supposed to say nothing."

Her mother hadn't considered that Tracy would blame Leanne, or that Tracy's mother would be so upset, she'd be determined to set it right for Leanne. It was Tracy's mother who came up with the idea of highlights.

"It will be our present," Tracy's mother said. "I'm working that day, and I'll keep a couple of hours free for her." She grabbed Leanne's mother's arm and said, "You could get a pedicure first and make a day of it."

When she saw the doubt on Leanne's mother's face, she said, "You can't let him scare you. He sounds like a pure bully."

"He's unpredictable," Leanne's mother said, and missed the glance that Tracy threw at Leanne.

"We're all unpredictable sometimes," Tracy's mother said.

The following day, her mother stood outside Leanne's door and heard Tracy tell Leanne that she had to stand up to her parents. She was thirteen and everyone knew thirteen wasn't too young for make-up and hairdressers. Tracy's father let her do what she wanted because her mother told him that she wasn't a baby anymore. "And you're not a baby either. They can't keep acting weird just because something happened a hundred years ago."

Leanne's thinking of getting highlights tomorrow, a present from Tracy's mom.

They were sitting in Tracy's kitchen. The table was messy with wine glasses and tumblers of coke. Leanne had been against sending the text at first. "He'll just say no, so what's the point?"

But her mother argued that he could at least get used to the idea and that would be better than giving him a shock.

It took another five minutes to decide on the wording. It was late evening, and their reflections on the double glass door showed their attention was on the phone. The television was on in the living room. They heard a blast of gunfire and under it the beep of an alert. "That was fast," Leanne's mother said.

No way! Too Young!

"He said no way."

"He didn't even think about it," Tracy's mother said.

Leanne's mother said, "See what I mean."

Leanne said, "But what can he do?"

Everyone looked at her, and Tracy was the first to laugh.

"He'll be raging," Leanne's mother said.

Leanne told her that he never stayed mad for long when it was just him and her. When she'd worn the eye shadow, he'd ordered her to wash it off. She'd cried for an hour, and he'd apologized again and again.

Tracy's mother said, "He can't stay mad if you have a good argument ready for him."

She shouted at her son to turn the blasted television down.

Leanne's mother said, "Will I text him and tell him you've made up your mind?"

Her voice had lowered, and Leanne knew she'd hurt her when she insinuated that her father's anger was her mother's fault.

Leanne said, "No, leave him alone."

She started playing with the spoon in the sugar bowl, lifting it up and letting the grains fall. The television had been lowered, and Tracy's mother was back.

"So what will she say?" Tracy asked.

Tracy's mother said, "Tell him highlights are much better than overall dyes. And bleaches have no ammonia."

"Tell him I bought the present, and we couldn't get a refund," Tracy said.

"Good one," Leanne said, and stopped playing with the spoon.

"Tell him you won't get it done again until your next big birthday at sixteen," Leanne's mother said.

"Tell him if he likes it, I can do his too," Tracy's mother said. Tracy nudged her and told her not to be so stupid. "Tell him it's not alcohol."

"Or drugs…"

"I'll tell him I'm not a baby. I'm thirteen."

The next morning, no one had time to think about the father. Leanne and Tracy woke late after staying up past 3a.m chatting. They had to rush to get ready for the beauticians. Leanne sat between Tracy and her mother and hot water gushed at their feet. Her mother was quieter than normal and read magazines, while Leanne and Tracy nudged each other about articles and took selfies and whispered about how jealous their friends were going to be on Monday. Leanne picked a red varnish for her feet and peach for her hands. Waiting for the nails to dry, she sat close to Tracy at the window. Tracy said she couldn't wait to see her hair done. Leanne said, "Me too," and forgot the unease she'd been feeling because of her mother's reserve. She refused to think about going to her father's after this and was relieved when her mother livened up enough to ask where they should have lunch. They arrived at the hairdressers at 2.30p.m, but had to wait fifteen minutes.

Leanne had never been particularly vain, though she had started to notice that her face had a nice shape with high cheek bones and a narrow chin. When her mother said Leanne was beautiful, she believed her in a way that she would if her mother said it was raining outside. But that day, with Tracy's mother pulling her hair back and the silver foil going on, she felt as if she was seeing herself for the first time. The face was not a young girl's face anymore. She liked her eyes and the way they gazed outward, the seriousness of them played down by her smile. On that hairdresser's chair, she watched her transformation and the whole world disappeared except for her and Tracy, whose mother had to chastise her for jumping around. "Sit still or I'll send you outside."

It was 5:20 p.m. when they left the hairdressers. Her mother saw the father's missed calls and told Leanne to text him that she was on her way. "He knew we were running late," Leanne said, "Why is he so impatient?"

She texted *see you soon Dad.*

The silence of no reply got to her mother. She'd already phoned and told him that they were delayed, and they'd be at his house by 5:40 p.m. She'd called Leanne's gran at 2.30 as well to let her know so dinner wouldn't be ruined. It was a clear day and warmer than usual. Her mother was beginning to sweat by the time she got to the car.

"He'll like it, won't he?" Leanne said, once they'd started out of town.

Her mother parked in front of the father's house and stared at it for a second, before turning to Leanne.

"I'll see you tomorrow," Leanne said. She was light with the new image of her staring from the mirror, and she wanted to ignore her mother's worried expression.

"Should I walk in with you?"

Leanne thought it was bad enough that they were late. She couldn't go to the door with her mother in tow, and said "No, I'll be fine."

"But Leanne…"

"Mum, don't okay, I'll be fine." She reached over to hug her mother and whispered thanks.

Usually, her mother's car started by the time Leanne reached the gate, but the engine was still off, and now her mother was making Leanne nervous. Her steps were slow. The excitement she'd felt in the hairdressers and the car was seeping out of her. Leanne wished she could turn around and run back to the car, but she couldn't. She was pulled forward. At the door, she looked behind at her mother. She must have taken it as a signal to leave, because the purr of the engine rose, and she waved goodbye just as the door opened.

Did her mother see that correctly? She'd waved and her daughter was still looking at her. The front door opened and a pale hand pulled her daughter in. Leanne was gone, and her mother started to tremble with the thought of a different front door. The photo of the aunt had come to her like a slap in the face, so sudden and shocking that it felt as if the image had come from somewhere beyond her. She realized that her ex-husband must have thought of that photo when he saw his thirteen-year-old. Or, he must have been thinking of it all day, regretting over and over what had happened and what he didn't do. And the mother understood of course this was the case, because he was a man who dwelt in the past. It was easier to focus on past mistakes than think of the new ones he was making. "Regret takes no fucking effort," she'd told him before they separated, but she'd learned that this was not true. Regret could eat you from the inside out and twist you into someone else.

While they were at the hairdressers, he would have been in his dark house remembering the click of that camera and his sister's hand coming down from her face and her nudge.

"Walk with me," she'd said, "Come on, it's my birthday," or she might have said, "Come on, I don't want to walk alone."

He'd said no, even when his mother said, "Go on and walk with your sister."

He'd said no, and his sister was found naked in the woods days later.

A horn blasted when her mother pulled to the side of the road. The driver screamed something as he went by, but the mother didn't notice. She was starting to cry. That hand had darted out and pulled her daughter inside. He must have been standing at the living room window watching her approach and he must have noticed the highlights.

What had he been thinking about — his dead sister or the ugly world that made him lash out sometimes? He'd hit the mother once in the kitchen. She'd been a little drunk, a little handy with him and he'd told her to stop. She hadn't, and he'd hit her. The end had started there, though neither of them had realized it.

She turned the car around and drove back the the house. The place was too still and quiet. Her heart had quartered and separated; it had taken up every part of her chest. She nearly tripped when she was getting out of the car. Her high heels made her want to scream while she ran up the path. His front door wasn't locked. She heard her daughter crying before she fell into the living room and ran towards the two forms, one pulling the other. The father had the daughter by the hair and the mother shouted at him to let go, without noticing the scissors glinting silver in the dim light. Later, trembling and pale-faced, his stomach reeling with the intimacy of her flesh, he would say the mother ran into him. She wouldn't remember how it happened. One second she was running and shouting, and the next she was on the floor with a sharp pain sweeping through her belly, while next door the grandmother rose from her seat and went to the window. She was sure she'd seen something in the yard, a slight figure running away, but there was only a deep still silence.

What It Is To Be Empty-Handed

I DIDN'T SLEEP MUCH because of the article. I couldn't stop thinking of the bus station with the high ceilings and hard wooden benches and the woman sitting with her baby, only she wasn't really a woman. She wasn't much older than I was and that made me feel empty inside. I hated to think about what happened and how everything turned so badly for her and her baby. The woman had three other children since that bus station, and the article said she lived in Ohio, but I imagined her somewhere warm, Florida or California, with sunshine streaming through the window. She was not in a grey place like Boston with snow on the ground and freezing weather that had a knack of finding you inside.

Her husband held her hand while she was being interviewed, and said he didn't blame her for what happened, though she was stupid and naïve, and I couldn't help hating her a little for it. But I wasn't really angry until I heard Debra come in. It was starting to get bright when she opened my door. She whispered my name, and I closed my eyes and was afraid of what I might say if she came any closer. Some nights, she liked to sit on the bed and talk about the customers from the diner. Sometimes, one of them would be waiting for her in the living room. Once, I went to the bathroom in the middle of the night and I ran into one of those men. I was in my underwear and he blocked the bathroom door. Debra woke to me crying. Ever since then, she shook me awake if she had company and warned me to put on some clothes if I wanted to go to the bathroom.

I was still getting used to calling her Debra. Days after our last move, she'd decided she didn't want to be called Mom anymore. The first I heard of it was when she said the boys next door introduced themselves to her. She told them her name was Debra and she lived with a roommate. She said there was no reason for them to question her since she looked young and I looked older than my years because of my height and my serious way of looking at the world. It felt as if she was getting smaller and smaller when she was saying this. If I reached out, there would be nothing but air.

"They seem nice," Debra said about the boys next door. "They said we could visit for a drink any time."

I said no way. I was not going next door with Debra, to be ignored while the boys fumbled around her. A few days later, when the next door neighbor knocked on our door, I assumed he wanted Debra. I said she was looking for a job and then I wished I hadn't volunteered so much information. It made me sound childish.

"I didn't come here to see her," the neighbor said. He wasn't much taller than me and had narrow shoulders. He was wearing stained jeans and a cap that was low on is head so it was hard to see his eyes. He seemed shy. After a few seconds, he smiled and asked if he could come in. I said no. He nodded and said, 'okay', in a way that made me feel sorry for him. He came back a few times after that. When he was on his way to get some food, he stopped to ask if I wanted any and he arrived with a packet of biscuits from the store across the street, always when Debra was out, but he didn't ask if he could come in again.

The morning after reading the article, I kept thinking of that girl and her baby. I was waiting for Debra to wake so I could talk to her, but she was sprawled on her bed in her clothes. It was already 4 p.m., and she was probably missing work but I couldn't wake her because then she'd be angry. I'd have to listen to her talk about her annoying customers or how hard it was to stay on her feet all night and how she deserved to go out and have a life. I'd want to tell her about that woman in Ohio, who said she'd lost her heart in the middle of a bus station and no one could do anything. But Debra would probably ask that means, and I wouldn't be able to tell her the whole story.

Outside was cold. The pavement was sprinkled with snow and the wind cut my cheeks. I didn't know where I was going until I closed the door. Then, I remembered my neighbor bringing me gifts and asking if he could come in, and I imagined he'd smile when he saw me.

He was older than I thought he was. Without the cap, I noticed his hair was receding and his forehead was broad. He was surprised to see me and it took a second before he smiled so I had an urge to run, but I didn't want to look like a baby. It was me who rang the bell, though I had to concentrate to remember what I wanted to say.

"Hey there," he said. "Come in."

He stepped back and I followed. The dark hall was cluttered with boots. I nearly tripped. He said sorry for the mess. He meant to clean it up, but…and then he stopped talking. He might have shrugged, but I didn't see. He was around the same height as me and his arms were wiry and strong looking. He was barefoot.

"I thought you might be working today," I said.

The living room was gloomy. Clothes were on the couch and the floor. He picked them up and threw them into one of the other rooms without stepping inside. An ashtray was on the table. The television was on with the volume muted. There was a car chase going on. He said he was owed a few days holiday and he decided to take it today. He said it was hard working outside in the cold. I asked what he did and he said I was a curious bee, which made me nervous because I didn't know if I could ask any more questions. I wished he'd open the blinds and that he'd left the movie on. Without the distraction, I felt too big in this room. It was hard to move, as if I'd crawled into a cave. He was watching me with a smile and I said it was very dark. It was a relief when he apologized and opened the blinds half-way. The living room was at the back of the apartment. There were two doors on the left which were probably the bedrooms. We'd passed the kitchen on the way. I'd glimpsed dishes in the sink and the corner of a table. I didn't think his roommate was in.

"My name's Robert, did Debra tell you that? Most people call me Bob."

"Hi Bob."

I was not sure why he laughed, but I felt proud that I'd made him. When he asked my name, I told him Ashley. I hadn't realized I was going to lie until it came out. Lying was like that; it surprised you sometimes.

"Sit down Ashley, make yourself comfortable."

He pointed to the couch. The seat was so low and soft, I felt like I was being sucked in. He offered a drink, and I said, "Yeah sure, thanks."

There was a smell of cigarettes and musty clothes. I asked if he had any vodka and he said sorry no vodka, but he had some gin if that was ok.

I said yeah thanks.

The drink was strong. I tried not to make a face when I took a sip. He sat down so close our legs touched. He'd put on some music before he got the drinks. There was a guitar and a male singer but I didn't know what he was singing. I didn't want to ask who it was, because he might have said something like where have you been the last ten years and ten years ago I was four.

Bob started talking about the band. He asked if I liked them and I said yeah sure, and he said he saw them in concert not long ago and that they were great and had so much energy. He didn't know how they did it. He asked what music I liked, and I told him I listened to anything but I liked jazz, which wasn't necessarily a lie. I'd heard jazz once or twice and it was okay, but I said it because it sounded good. He smiled in a weird way and said that I'd have to shoot him before he'd listen to that, which didn't make sense. If I shot him, he'd be dead, though maybe he meant wound him badly.

He was drinking beer out of a can and he drank deeply. I could have probably counted to ten, and then he wiped his lips and got up and asked if I wanted another.

"Not yet," I said.

He said, "Don't be a lightweight."

His hard stare reminded me of Debra and I wanted him to stop so I drank the gin down. I coughed afterwards and he laughed. The ice clicked against the side of the glass. My head felt woozy and light. I sat back and closed my eyes. I heard the fridge open and close, and then nothing and I woke to his hand on my leg. He was handing me the drink and I had a sense of floating that I wanted to hold onto for as long as I could.

The gin felt thick in my mouth. Bob was probably the

same age as Debra. It was hard to tell in this light. He tapped his foot to the music and asked if I had a boyfriend.

I said, "No."

He said, "Good."

The baby's name was Emma. I'd tried it out that morning. I'd looked in the mirror and said. "Hello I'm Emma," a few times, but it didn't fit me. Emma suited a fragile girl with blonde hair, a girl who was shy and worked in an office. Emma didn't drink. She was offended by the bars and the people she saw propped up inside. I used to be scared of those places as a kid.

Once a woman stopped to ask if I was okay and I still remember her round cheeks and soft eyes. "I'm waiting," I told her. She was looking behind me. The door was open so we could hear voices. She asked who I was waiting for and I didn't want to answer her. I didn't like the way she was look- ing through that door. I wanted to grab her to stop her from going inside, but I couldn't move. There was shouting and then Debra stormed out of the bar and nearly yanked my arm from its socket when she pulled me down the street.

"What did I tell you about talking to strangers?" she said.

"You're very lovely Ashley," Bob said.

I felt the weight of his hand pressing into my leg. He said he hadn't stopped thinking of me since the first day he saw me. The gin made me a little sick. He asked where I used to live and I told him I came all the way from Ohio. I imagined that woman with the sad eyes writing me a letter, asking how everything was. I imagined she'd say how much she missed me and that she'd never stopped thinking of me, and I told Bob about my younger brother and two younger sisters who were coming to visit soon.

"Are you in college?" he asked. I said yeah. I didn't know if I liked the way he was looking at me. It was too fierce. He had a scar on his eye that I touched and he flinched as if it was raw, and said something about an accident. He changed the subject quickly, and said something about school or studying that was hard to catch. He downed his beer before asking if I wanted another and it was hard to think straight. There was gin in my glass but he was taking it again. I wondered what kind of accident he'd had, but by the time he'd gotten to the door, I'd forgotten what I was wondering about. I was thinking of Debra waking in the quiet apartment with a sore head.

My phone was off, but I imagined her pressing the call button again and again getting angrier by the minute. Debra hated being alone, that was why she insisted on homeschooling, though our bursts of work never lasted long. Whenever I disappeared before she woke, I had to stay out long enough that she'd be so relieved with my arrival she'd forget to be angry.

"It's an anniversary," I told Bob when he got back. I noticed he'd spilled some beer on his jeans and his nails were dirty. He looked confused. "Today, that's why I didn't go to classes. My mother nearly lost me."

He said yeah in the way people did when they weren't interested or weren't really listening.

"I listened to you talk about that stupid band," I said. His jaw got tight and his hand pressed on my leg. He leaned closer so I smelled his sour breath and unwashed hair. "What did you say?"

"It happened in a bus station," I said.

His eyes narrowed. His neck was loose, like a chicken's squawking neck. I wanted to laugh, but I couldn't, because the bus station was in my head again, and the woman with the baby swaddled up nice and warm. I wanted to tell Bob that the woman was only eighteen and it was her first time traveling a long distance. I couldn't remember where she came from, a family home? Loads of sisters and brothers? But I knew she was going to the baby's father. He'd gone ahead to settle them into a house, not the house they were in now, a smaller house, but one with a garden where the baby would have played, if the baby had arrived with her.

Bob was saying something but it was hard to focus. His mouth was hard and red. His arm went around me and I pulled away. I had to rub the tears from my cheeks. He sighed.

"She lost me," I said. "I was a baby and she lost me."

He asked what the fuck I was talking about.

"Her husband said it wasn't her fault, but how can anyone be so stupid? He said she was tired after her long journey, and still had another ten hours to go. She was young too, nearly as young as I am now. Could you imagine me with a baby?"

He didn't answer.

"A woman called Melanie came and sat beside her. At least that's what she called herself. Melanie sounds like a nice person, doesn't it? She sounds like a person who takes care of herself."

Bob's hand was moving on my leg.

"She wasn't a nice person, though she must have looked like one then. When I was a baby she wouldn't have been twenty yet and she probably didn't drink too much. She sat down and asked my mother's name, where she was going, what her husband did, and she talked about her own family. Then she asked if she could hold the baby."

Bob was watching me with that fierce gaze and I didn't want to look at him.

"The woman, Melanie, that's what her name was, she stood and said the baby needed a nappy change, and my mother said no, wait, because she was worried, but just for a second because she was so tired. "It's okay," Melanie said, "you need to rest.""

Bob told me to finish my drink and I did. He took the glass off me and I waited for him to ask what happened next.

I wanted to say that the woman saw Melanie going for the door of the station and she screamed 'she has my baby' and everyone jumped into action and stopped her. Melanie didn't make it into the dark street where she and the baby were swallowed up and lost because thirty years ago there were no videos to show what the woman looked like. There were no Internet or Facebook posts going viral. She just disappeared and probably moved from one crappy apartment to the other and homeschooled the girl so no questions would be asked, but I couldn't finish the story. I couldn't get beyond the bus station and the woman sitting there empty-handed.

CRASHING

Every Tuesday Catherine drove into town to clean the house for her son. The new dog meant she had to clean her house before she went too. It was Dermot who wanted to get a Terrier. Catherine tried to talk him out of it. She said it would be more work, and she hadn't even thought of the dog shedding hair all over the place or that every morning at the crack of dawn the dog would be yapping at their bedroom door. Dermot said a dog would get him out walking and get him up in the morning. She should never have believed that. Dermot was never an early riser in all the years she'd been married to him. With all that had to be done, Catherine had started to dread Tuesdays. She was sorry she didn't ignore the phone ringing Monday night when she was on her way to bed. She might have if Dermot hadn't shouted, "Are you going to get that?"

She said hello.

"Hey Ma," her son said. "You wouldn't bring some home-cooking tomorrow, would you? I'm getting fed up with fast food."

"Oh, it's so late. You should have asked me earlier," she said.

"I didn't think it was a bother. I didn't think you'd mind cooking something for your son every now and again."

His voice had risen like it used to when he was a boy and got upset. She felt guilty and a little appalled, but she apologized for upsetting him. It wasn't going to help his pain. He'd had one surgery for a prolapsed disc and might have to have another one soon.

She said of course, she'd bring something in. When she hung up, she stood in the dark hall for several seconds and heard Dermot laugh at something on TV

Her day had been planned to the last minute, and now everything had to be changed. Instead of buying the Chicken Kiev on the way home for dinner, she had to defrost the beef overnight and make a stew, which would take at least an hour off her morning. Then she was struck with the idea that there might not be enough beef and it would probably be best to bring the whole pot to her son and get the Chicken Kiev anyway, which meant cooking two dinners and she hated cooking two dinners in the one day.

These thoughts kept going around in her head, so it must have been after midnight when she finally drifted off to sleep.

When she woke, the dog was yapping in the hallway and Dermot was sound asleep. He slept like he'd been knocked out, like waking up he had to come back from the darkest reaches of the world. She'd never known anyone to sleep like him. Her mother used to say it was because he was bone lazy and sleep was his natural way of being. She laughed when she said that. She thought Dermot harmless, even when he used to sit on a bar-stool until he couldn't sit anymore.

He'd phone Catherine for a lift and then take the chair in the living room and wait for his dinner to be put in front of him. But there was not a bit of harm to him, not like some of them out there, Catherine's Ma would say. Some of them being Catherine's Da who didn't drink, but had a temper that boiled through him. He was never still. Even watching television, he'd fidget around in the armchair, lighting cigarettes and shouting for tea, or looking for the paper and the keys to the car that he needed to have in plain sight always. Then he might start watching what was on and get annoyed with it. Catherine would feel the room warm up with his irritation and she learned to abandon whatever she was watching. Her mother would sometimes stay and shouting would ensue. Although there were never any hands raised, the shouting was scary because of the way his broad face scrunched up and spittle flew from his mouth.

Dermot never shouted. "Thanks for the tea," he'd say to Catherine and he'd fall asleep on the armchair with the tray over his legs and gravy on his Sunday shirt.

He worked in a garage, but he had a bad back too.

"It runs in the family," he'd said, when their son had to have surgery, though there was never any prolapsed disc with Dermot.

There was nothing that the doctors could point out on the x-ray and try to fix. His pain was muscular and it made working as a mechanic hard, because of all the lying down and lifting. He had to give it up when their son was in secondary school.

He gave up drink around that time after a visit to the hospital from crippling pains in his belly. He had blood taken and tests done. The doctor was a small Indian man with a stare that filled the room. He stood at the side of the bed and asked how much Dermot drank in a day. Dermot said not too much and the doctor looked at him as if he was a child who said horses could fly.

"Keep it up and you'll last ten years at most, maybe five."

The doctor apologized to Catherine, who was sitting on the chair by the bed, and she had no idea why, until he said that as far as he was concerned her husband was taking up a bed that people with real medical problems needed.

"He should shoot himself. It would be easier and less expensive," the doctor said in such a serious, expressionless manner that all Catherine could do was nod and say okay.

Dermot was discharged and he went straight to bed when he got home. He didn't go to the bar the next night or the next and Catherine was sure it was because he didn't want to ever see that doctor again.

The dog was scratching the door.

"Dermot, the dog needs to be taken out," Catherine was sitting on her side of the bed. The rain pattered against the window and she felt a heavy gloom when he didn't respond. She put a hand on his side. He was curled up like a child.

Sometimes she was sure he could hear her. She'd imagine him smiling with his eyes closed. Now she didn't want to imagine him smiling or awake because it made her feel helpless. The dog was yapping and scratching at the door and if they didn't bring him out soon, he'd probably pee in the house.

"Dermot please," she said, "I've got to get the stew on."

He moaned something incomprehensible. She gave him a shake. He'd grown thin in the last years. She was struck with the notion that she could blow him off the bed, and this saddened her.

"Dermot, please," she said.

"It'll be okay," he mumbled.

She didn't know if he meant the dog or the fact that she had to do the stew. She did know that she could spend several more minutes shaking him and pleading for him to get up and it would do no good. With the curtains opened to let in the bits of stray light, she got dressed.

The rain on her face surprised her for the cold. It was April and she never knew what it would be like when she stood outside. She should have worn a hat and gloves, but the dog had hardly given her enough time.

She walked the dog to the small green across the way that separated her house from the smaller bungalows and where her son and his friends used to play. Other children played there now, but it was quiet in the early morning. It was not yet time for the children to leave their houses with their parents to walk hand-in-hand to the primary school or to saunter in groups to the secondary school.

The dog peed straight away, but Catherine had to walk around the green twice before it did the other business and she said under her breath, "Oh come on now," and pulled hard at its leash, and then felt guilty and had to bend down and pet it and get muddy from its paws.

Dermot was still in bed when she got back to the house. She dried the dog, and thought that she'd have to peel the whole bag of spuds because her son was a demon for potatoes. He liked the carrots too. He'd complain if he put a ladle into the saucepan and it didn't come up full of vegetable and meat. He'd say he thought it was a stew not soup.

Once, when Catherine had said that was exactly what was before him, he'd actually looked up the definition of stew and showed her that it was a dish of meat and vegetable cooked slowly in liquid.

"See," he'd said, "Cooked in liquid, not swimming in it."

The floor above her creaked with Dermot's rising. She'd finished peeling the fifth spud and she cut it up and wiped her hands on her apron before putting on the kettle and heating the pan to fry his egg. He liked his egg soft, put a fork in it and it should flow like melted gold, he liked to say.

The bacon and sausages were only on the weekends. When their son was young, the Saturday fry up was one of Catherine's favorite meals. They'd sit around the table with a mountain of pig and toast and refill one teapot after another and talk about their week or what was on at the weekend and anything else that might come up.

Saturdays saddened her now and so did the sound of the

kids playing, especially on a summer evening with all the windows open and the freshness in the air. She'd be hit with the silence in her house, the room upstairs not being used anymore, and all the time that had slipped away.

Dermot came into the kitchen rubbing his hands. A strand of his brown hair was sticking up at the back of his head, "My belly woke me up, I swear to God, I heard it growling in my sleep."

Then he stood by the range that emitted a soft heat from the fire and said he might need two eggs today, since he was trying to cut down on the bread. The dog was lying on its bed by the range. It was quiet now, and he watched Dermot without raising his head. Catherine got a kick out of him when he did things like that. The dog appeared to be snubbing Dermot for not walking him.

"I think he's mad you didn't walk him," she said.

Dermot scoffed and said he doubted any such thing. "Is there tea brewing?"

Dermot was having a cigarette and re-reading some of the papers from yesterday. Catherine had decided after she'd peeled all the vegetables and fried the beef till it was brown that it would be better to bring it to her son's house as it was. Then she could boil up the stock and have the stew cooking while she cleaned. Her son's house was a shock every week. It was hard to know how so much dust and dirt could accumulate in so little time. Her son always apologized, "I'm sorry Ma," he'd say, "But it was a really bad week. I could hardly stand."

He was thirty-three, the age of Christ when he died, and Catherine felt bad for his suffering so young.

She felt terrible that sometimes she'd park the car and not want to go into his dark house where the curtains were still drawn at 11 o'clock and there was a smell of something gone off that she could never find the source of. It could be the laundry or the food in the kitchen or the lack of air in the bathroom. Usually, she couldn't detect it once she was done cleaning. A couple of times when he wasn't home, she stepped out of the house for a few moments and stepped back in to see if she'd just gotten accustomed to the smell while she'd worked. She could never be sure if this was the case.

She always started in the kitchen with the dishes that would be left for a few nights and then the shelves and windows and floors. He didn't use the cooker much but the microwave made up for that. Then there was the downstairs bathroom that she instructed him to bleach at least twice a week so it would be easier for her back too. He promised that he always did it, but one week she'd left an empty bottle of bleach by the toilet and there was no new one the next week and still he said he'd bleached the place.

While she was cleaning the bathroom and the living room, the meat and carrots would be stewing. Before she went upstairs to his bedroom and the second bathroom that took longer because of the bath, which he used every night on account of his back, she'd have the potatoes on. It was a relief to have it all worked out, but an aggravation that she was still nearly an hour late setting off because of the preparation. Her son had called her twice already to ask where she was.

The day hadn't brightened. A steady rain was falling onto the windscreen. Catherine didn't like driving in the rain. The splattering of drops on all sides made her feel hemmed in and tiny, and she tended to lean forward with her chin nearly over the steering wheel. The tension would send shooting pains around her shoulders.

Her house was five miles from the town and her son. A new motorway with three lanes of traffic had been built, but she'd only driven on it once and would never do it again. She preferred the old road and didn't care about being stuck behind a tractor or sharp bends that forced you to slow down to thirty miles an hour.

The bend by the Daly house was the worst. An octogenarian, Mags Daly lived up the hill from there and had been writing to the council for years to get the road widened but nothing had been done. The new motorway meant it was unlikely to get done now.

Catherine thought about taking the motorway, because she couldn't stand any further delay, but she took too long to put her indicator on and there was someone behind her. There was no choice but to continue onto the old road. She kept going over in her head what she had to do; clean the kitchen first and then put the pot on, and then rush to the bathroom. She might have looked at the pot with all the food that she'd set in the passenger seat. She might have reached a hand out to make sure it was steady and would not fall, but then she was looking back on the road.

The rain was falling in slants and the trees were heavy with water. There was a sudden flash of movement. His face was before her, and then she felt the thud and the sound of her scream filled her head.

The wipers went over and back. Potatoes and carrots were on the floor beside her. She turned off the engine. Every part of her was trembling. She had to phone 911 to report an accident before she could get out and see what that was, but she knew what it was. She'd seen his face, the pale skin and blonde hair, the flash of a man there one moment, and gone the next as if a great big hole had opened under him.

She was surprised her voice sounded the same when she told the emergency worker that someone was hurt on the old road at the Daly bend. She was slow getting out, but when she saw his body, she ran until her legs gave way with the shock and she fell onto the wet ground.

He'd been thrown to near the middle of the road and his body was twisted in a strange way. The legs were folded up, as if he was on his side, but he was lying on his back with his face to the sky. There was blood all down his cheeks and a great gash in his head. She wanted to scream at the rain to leave him alone. It pelted his face that looked so young. He was not yet a man. She could feel his youth, as if it was a shining thing around him and she knew she shouldn't move him. She'd seen it on TV enough that it was best to let the medics take care of him, but she couldn't let the rain fall on him like that. On her knees, she held the side of him and pulled him to her.

She wiped his face and the warmth of his skin made her cry out. The blood kept coming out of the hole in his head. She kept cleaning him with her cardigan. She wanted to see his face. He didn't look upset or angry. His mouth was held in a soft line. There was no alarm and she couldn't let the blood take that away from him.

"It'll be okay," she said. She felt the warmth fading and she hugged him to her and said, "No, don't, they'll be here soon, please don't go."

They found her on her knees hugging him. Her clothes soaked from the rain and blood and when they tried to take him, she fought them, and tried to keep him close. To him, she said, "No, it'll be okay."

She was sobbing because she knew it wasn't okay. She'd held him as the warmth drained and she'd known he was gone before she'd heard the sirens and before the medics came rushing to her.

Yet she wanted to pretend it wasn't so, and if she could keep hold him for a little longer, she could pretend he was that warm shiny body she'd first seen. They eased her away. Faces would come back to her in the next few days, and she'd know they were the medics who held her arms softly and brought her to the ambulance.

"He was there all of a sudden," she said, while they checked her injuries.

At one stage, she threw the blanket from her and said

she needed to get to her son. The stew needed to be cooked, and the house. "You should see his house," she said. "He's in pain you see."

And she looked at the faces that would come back to her now and again, round cheeks and soft eyes, and she said, "Is he hurt? Will he be okay?"

They had to sedate her when she tried to get up a second and third time. She was brought home, though she'd remember little of the journey. She wouldn't remember Dermot bringing her upstairs and helping her shower, or sitting in the kitchen with some tea for a long time without drinking any. The car was taken from the scene and Dermot phoned her son. He asked to speak to her and she was brought to the phone in her nightdress. Every now and again, she'd be hit with a fit of trembling and she'd remember the boy's face.

"Are you okay, Ma?"

She said, "Yes, I'll be okay."

It didn't sound like her, but like a voice that had been buried deep inside her. She thought it was muffled, but her son didn't say anything.

He asked if she wanted him to come out.

She said, "No, driving's not good for your back. I'll see you tomorrow."

In bed, she closed her eyes, and she saw the boy, and she opened her eyes again and stared at the drawn curtains. She wished the rain would be louder, so the sound might take up space in her head and mute out his face and the stillness of him and the gentle mouth.

She slept on and off. Hers was a fitful sleep that never released her fully. It was like swimming, reaching the surface and falling back under water again. She didn't hear Dermot get in the bed beside her.

The dog woke her in the morning. Dermot was asleep and snoring lightly. She opened the curtains to see that the rain had stopped, though the day had an ashen quality to it. Her stomach was sick, and she was a little light-headed, and she put a hand on Dermot's side, but she didn't say his name. It got rooted in her stomach. For a moment she thought she'd cry, but it passed.

She dressed in a pair of black pants that were around-the-house clothes and a woolen cardigan. The dog was all over her when she opened the bedroom door and she told it to hush.

In the kitchen, she had a quick banana and put the kettle to boil. She nearly went out in her slippers, but she remembered in time.

Outside, the air was warmer than yesterday and she stood staring at her car. The left side was dented and the light was smashed. It made her conscious of her neighbors thinking she was the woman who'd hit the boy and cradled him and felt him being taken away.

Her legs went weak and she thought she might fall, but the dog was pulling her and she was going to the green where she walked in circles. She saw the arrival of the Garda car from there and stopped frozen.

They were in the kitchen-Dermot, in his jeans and t-shirt was barefoot. A female Garda was sitting at the table opposite him. A male Garda was standing by the range that wasn't lit yet. Catherine was behind today. The dog scampered into the kitchen to his bowls she'd filled with water and food earlier.

"There was a witness," the female garda said.

Catherine said oh.

The garda said Mrs. Daly had been watering the plants in her front room when she'd seen the Flynn boy walking from his house in the rain. The Flynn's lived on the same slip road as the Daly's and she knew the boy hadn't been in school for a few weeks. There was something with the boy she thought wasn't right, but it took several moments before she realized he wasn't wearing a jacket and he didn't seem aware of the rain. She was still watching him, when he came to the main road and stopped. He looked to the left, and then stepped back.

The garda stopped talking. Catherine said go on.

Mrs. Daly said she saw the car coming. There was a flash of color, but her attention was on the boy and she didn't think anything about the car until seconds before it happened, when she knew he was going to run out.

The male garda said, "It wasn't your fault. He ran out in front of you on purpose."

"I nearly went on the motorway, but there was a car behind me," Catherine said.

"Then it would have been someone else."

Catherine couldn't imagine anyone else on that road with him. No one would have held him like she did.

"See it wasn't your fault. There was nothing you could have done," Dermot said, when the gardai were gone. He'd lit a cigarette, and had opened the back door to let out the smoke. The dog was in his bed.

"It's a shocking thing to do to anyone," Dermot said. "Pure selfish."

She closed her eyes and saw the wet corner of the road and she couldn't think of the boy as selfish. It was fear, she thought. He didn't want to go alone.

She cracked the egg into the pot and saw the perfection of it, the single yoke caught in the white. The pot from yesterday was on the stove and all the food inside. Dermot said he'd picked everything from the floor yesterday. He said there was some mess, but he made sure to wash all the vegetables thoroughly and he threw out the beef.

Catherine thanked him because it seemed expected. He said he'd also washed the car and checked to make sure nothing was wrong. He didn't say anything when the egg was put before him a little hard. He stared at it for a few seconds before pushing the plate away and she went to the fridge to get another one.

She didn't go to her son's house that day or the next. The neighbors called. Nollaig from across the green came with a troubled face and pie. She wouldn't let Catherine make the tea.

"Sit down you," she said, "It's an awful shock."

With the teapot between them, she asked how Catherine was.

"I don't know," Catherine said and this was true. She might be doing something like making the beds or making the dinner, and she'd feel his body in her arms and she wouldn't know how she was in her house. Sometimes, she didn't know how to continue. It was like pushing through a wall.

Sara from next door arrived, and said her son had gone to school with the boy. They'd been friends and she wanted to know what happened, if he'd really jumped out. Catherine took Sara into the kitchen and told her how fast it all happened. One minute, there was nothing and then his face, but she couldn't tell her about holding the boy in her arms and begging him to stay.

Catherine heard the funeral notice on the radio and had to sit down. She'd been expecting to hear it, since it was why she'd put on North-West radio to begin with, but still to hear his name aloud made the ground slip from under her. He was eighteen years of age.

Friday, on the way to her son's house, she took the motorway. She wanted to take the old road, to drive that patch without the rain, but if she went that way she was afraid she'd stop at the bend and not go any further. Maybe, she was still sitting there on the cold asphalt and he hadn't left. Then she remembered the removal was on that day. She'd thought of going and it was another thing she couldn't do, not from the shame of it, but from the intimacy. She'd want to touch him, to reach out and lift him up, to cry over him again and she was afraid of that need.

Her son's house was a compact two-story with the door opening up onto the street and a small patch of garden at back. She had the key in the door when her son opened it. He was tall and he used to be thin but there was extra weight on his cheeks and his belly flowed over his jeans. He kissed her cheek and she smelt cigarettes. "Hi Ma," he said, "Good to see you."

He took the pot from her hands and led her into the kitchen, which was the worst she'd ever seen it. Dishes were piled high and she could see the stickiness on the table. She stopped at the door while he put the pot on the cooker. She hadn't been able to cook the stew at home. There were little ways to keep the boy with her. When she put the pot in the car, she thought of him walking down his road.

Her son was putting on his jacket. He said he had an appointment with the doctor and he'd be back as soon as he could. She'd browned the beef already, and now she boiled it in stock with the carrots. Then she stood still in the room. Her son hadn't asked about the boy. He was eighteen, she would have told him, so young, remember you at eighteen, the world ahead of you.

The dishes were caked and hard, and her arm hurt from scrubbing the table. She cleaned on autopilot, as something she needed to do, but she felt as if she wasn't really there. She was watching herself scrub the dishes and open the door to let in the blast of air.

The stew was boiling for minutes before she realized she hadn't turned it to simmer. She had to scrape the meat from the bottom.

The bathroom downstairs wasn't too bad. Still, she was

slower than usual. The boy wouldn't let her rest. On her knees in the bathroom upstairs, she remembered the hard road under her and the stone digging into her skin with his weight resting on her. When they'd lifted him off her, she couldn't stand. Her legs were a dead weight under her.

Her face in the mirror seemed wrong. She sprayed Windex on the glass and wiped it with a paper towel. It was like an unveiling with the spray being rubbed off to see her face, only it wasn't her. By the third unveiling, she realized it was her eyes. They looked at her differently which confused her, because, if the eyes looked at her differently, wasn't she different? Wasn't it a new mouth, a new chin, raised upward, because she would have fought, if it had meant something? If it could have brought him back for even five more seconds, she would have clawed at them and this was in her face now, but not all the time. Other times she didn't remember the fright as much as the pain and the shock, and the way she'd crawled to him on hands and knees.

She was upstairs when her son came back and shouted, "Hello Ma, something smells good."

She remembered the stew. The potatoes had been put in ages ago; she couldn't remember when. Her son was taking off his jacket. He was smiling until he saw her. A stocky middle-aged woman in her sweatpants gripping the bannister and looking like she might topple forward because she was trying to go that fast.

"Are you alright, Ma?"

"The stew," she said.

"Ah Ma, I've been looking forward to that stew all week."

The potatoes were overcooked mush and she stood by the pot staring in. He came beside her and sighed.

"He was eighteen, did you know that?" she said.

"You're lucky you weren't hurt," he said.

He asked if she was doing okay. She said sometimes. He nodded, and said he was sorry for it. After a while, he said he'd have a little of the stew. He took a plate out of the cupboard, a plate that she had washed and dried and put there, a plate that he might leave in the sink for her to wash next week, so it would be better to wait until he was done and clean it now.

On the way home, she'd have to get a piece of meat at the butchers. Dermot would not eat what she'd made. He'd walk into the kitchen and walk out again and he'd close the living-room door in anger. The television would be on, but if she wanted to watch, he'd tell her he needed to be alone.

"It's not so bad," her son said.

There was a faint smell of burning. The bottom of the pot would be ruined.

Saturday late morning, Catherine changed into a black skirt and blouse and left the house when Dermot took the dog out for a walk. She couldn't tell him she wanted to go to the funeral. He would have told her not to go. If ever she brought up the boy, he'd sigh with consternation, and say it was an awful thing for him to do, or he'd tell her he didn't like to think about what happened, so she never said how she'd held the boy. It hurt to hold it in.

She parked away from the church and waited until most of the people were gone inside before getting out of the car. A group of kids the boy's age, dressed in black dresses and pants remained outside talking. She wondered what he had been like before the walk to the main road, if he'd chatted as these kids. Two girls were talking alone and three boys were together. She was at the church gate when she saw one boy nudge another. She saw the first boy was Sara's son, Alby. The other boys were looking at her now. The girls had stopped talking and one turned to the boys. Catherine couldn't hear, but Alby must have said that's Catherine Molloy, the woman who hit him, because the girls were watching her now. Their faces had opened with a curious sympathy while the boys looked wary and unsure. She couldn't walk by those boys and turned back to the car. By the time she sat inside, the kids were gone.

Tuesday, she rose, as she had done for the previous weeks in a dazed stupor that made her feel she had not woken at all. She took the dog out to the green. There was slowness to her walk that was not from tiredness, but from the notion that she didn't know this place at all. Oh she knew it, the green and the houses and the school up the road and the quarry, but only the outline. She had no idea what it was like inside those houses. There were some she could imagine. Nollaig would be having breakfast with her daughter, and Sara would be shouting at her son to wake. But there were neighbors Catherine only knew to nod to. Their houses stood a stone throw from her home and she had no idea who they were and what they might be doing right now.

Sometimes the vastness of what she didn't know would overwhelm her, and she'd have to stop in the green and take deep breaths. It wasn't fear she felt then, or nerves. She imagined it was like an insect having the rock lifted from over them, stunned by the bright light, yet too ignorant to process it. She knew that the boy's house was on the hill on the slip road. There was the Daly house and then the blue bungalow that didn't face onto the road but faced towards town.

The afternoon of the funeral, unable to settle, she'd gone for a drive and it was the first time on the old road since the accident. She parked just beyond the bend. It was a long time before she got out of the car and walked to the road he'd come from. It was a narrow gravel road with high hedges, where he would have hidden behind.

Before she knew it, she was walking on that road. She knew the house immediately. The porch outside was made of glass. The garden was well-tended with flowers. The blueness of it, the quiet of it, it was where he'd come from. She stopped by a curve in the road, a perfect focal point, where she would not be seen. She didn't move until the front door opened and a body came out. She didn't wait to see if it was male or female.

She brought the dog home and fed and watered him.

With the sound of the floor above creaking with Dermot's footsteps, she got the pan out and heated it.

"Not a bad day out there," Dermot said.

He sat at the table, and if he was aware of her lack of reply, he said nothing of it. As always, he browsed through yesterday's papers while she put on the toast and made the tea. Every action was harder than the last, but she bore it because she didn't know how not to.

"Thanking you," he said, when the egg was before him. He pierced it with a fork and smiled. "How long will you be away?" he asked.

She said she didn't know. He laughed, and said, "It all depends what he has waiting for you."

She said, "Yes. I'll head off now though, so I won't be out all day."

She drove through the estate and over the bridge and through the village without any clear thought. Once she past the ramp for the motorway, her heart started to quicken and she had to grasp the steering wheel tight for the sweat in her hands.

She came to the corner and turned onto the slip road, and thought this is the car that took their boy. It still held the marks of his body. If she had considered this before, she wouldn't have gone, but it was too late now. The road was too narrow to turn around and someone might have seen her already. His mother might be at the front window watching her approach, and then to see the car turn would be dreadful for its cowardice.

Catherine parked the car by the low wall in front of their house. It was hard to breathe now. She was scared her heart might burst from her chest and she didn't know if she could walk. The trembling seemed to be in her blood. Her hands still gripped the steering wheel. What would she say if she went to their door? She hadn't thought of that. She'd thought of nothing except what the parents must want to know. She had no idea how to begin telling them.

The knock on the driver's door didn't alarm her, though it came again before she was able to look. She saw a man with a narrow face and deep wrinkles around his eyes. His brown hair was to his shoulder and turning grey.

"Catherine Molloy," he said. She nodded and tears came to his eyes. He thanked her for coming and said, "She wants you to come in."

He stepped back from the door to let her out and they stood on the side of the road, uncertain, but not uncomfortable. He was wearing dirty jeans and wellies. "I have things to attend to, but you go on. She's waiting for you."

The boy's mother was standing by the living room window. Catherine saw with a glance that she was in jeans and a sweater and had the same color hair as her son, but she could not meet the woman's gaze as she approached.

Catherine took the step to the front door. His mother was in the hall now. Her face was soft and Catherine wanted to run from the pain in her eyes, but his mother stepped forward and took Catherine's hand. She wasn't a tall woman,

"Thank you for coming," she said.

Catherine nodded. His mother's eyes were a pale blue and filled with tears.

Catherine followed her into the living room where a fire was lit. His mother motioned for Catherine to sit on the couch. She offered tea and Catherine said no. Now, in the house with the woman before her, all uncertainties had fled, but she was afraid if the mother left and made tea or if they skirted the real reason she was here, she might grow scared.

His mother sat beside her and said, "Tell me."

Catherine told her about the rain, and that she nearly took the motorway. She told her how fast he appeared, and how close he was, and she didn't have a chance to stop in time. She said, "He didn't look frightened."

His mother wiped her cheeks. They stared at the fire for a moment, before his mother said they were watching him all the time. There was always someone in the house, though he seemed okay that day. He asked her to make him a ham and cheese toasty, his favorite. That's what she was doing when he walked the road.

The fire spit out embers that fell against the fire-guard and dropped to the tiles of the fireplace to die out.

Catherine said, "I held him." She stopped, but the mother's hand squeezed hers and Catherine had to say it, no matter how much it hurt. "I held him, and I loved him like my own son."

His mother made a sound that tore at Catherine. Tears streamed down their faces and nothing was said for a long time. Finally, his mother rose and asked Catherine to follow her. She led Catherine down the hallway to the second door on the right. His mother opened it to a room with a single bed and posters on the wall.

She smiled at Catherine when her phone rang. Catherine took it out of her pocket and turned it off. The silence was a relief. Catherine could not say the caller was her son. She could not say that he was waiting for her in his house and that it was impossible to go to him. Inside the room, she saw a book lying face down on the bed, a hoody was on the floor and balled up papers had been tossed under the desk. Catherine imagined the boy sitting at his desk staring out at the rain and waiting to know the right things to write. She wondered if he'd found the words and if his mother had something to hold onto. Catherine thought maybe someday she'd ask, but not today.

Cold Spell

It was after 7 p.m. when I remembered the birthday cake for Miles. This was exactly the kind of stuff Nicola had complained about; me not being there to help when she was working full-time and taking care of our son. I'd told her that wasn't true and she'd said fine, I could organize the birthday party. She'd walked out of the room with her hands held high. Later, I told her to stop being so dramatic and she'd told me to stop being so absent. I couldn't have given her another reason to complain, so I had to drag myself away from the half-finished sentence glaring at me from the computer screen.

Stop-n-Shop was a fifteen minute walk. Nicola had taken the car to work. I'd sold mine when I started my PhD. I'd argued that the Mini should go. The Honda was better if we needed to go any distance. Nicola said no way. She'd said she loved her Mini and she couldn't get rid of it because it was a gift from her father.

Miles was focused on his video games. I could shout fire and he wouldn't move, which was another bone of contention with Nicola. She insisted any child would play games all day and it was our job not to let it happen. I told Miles I had to run out to the store and I'd be back in twenty minutes. He nodded, without taking his eyes off the screen. He was turning ten, and it was only in the last few weeks that I felt able to leave him to run an errand, but I'd never left him this late.

Outside, I smelled the sea and by the time I'd locked the door, I wished I brought my gloves. Over a foot of snow lay on the ground and the tree in our back yard was missing branches. It was a skinny tree, too thin for Miles to ever climb, but he used to love trying to reach the branches that were now broken and buried in the snow. At least, the weather made his party easier to organize. Usually, we had a barbecue in the back with his friends and the parents we liked. The previous year we had a magician, but now the garden was off-limits, so Miles and I decided he'd have some friends around and play video games and have pizza.

"That's it," Nicola said, when I told her.

I said, "That's what he wants."

We were about to have dinner. Nicola was bringing the bowl of pasta to the table, and she paused to look at me. I was grating the cheese and I thought here we go, but she just shrugged and went to the table. She sat, and didn't say anything and I wondered if she'd noticed there was no cake. She was on the evening shift and she'd been quiet all day. At one stage, I'd gone into the bedroom to find her curled on the bed.

I said her name and she didn't answer, but I could have sworn she was awake.

The beach close to the house was abandoned. The surface of the water was lit by city lights that spread from across the bay. A silver tint played on ripples. Street lights didn't reach as far as the tide, but it was enough for me to notice that there was a dark mass on the sand. The unease made me think of Miles in the house alone. There was an urge to run back to him, and yet I found myself standing rigid waiting for a car to pass before crossing the street. The murmur of the sea filled my ears. Behind me, another car went by and the headlights swept over the wet sand. Whatever was lying there had not moved.

A plane flew overhead, but I didn't look up from the biggest starfish I'd ever seen. I wondered when it had appeared and how a starfish of that size could go unnoticed. I thought of phoning Nicola and saying you'll never guess what I'm looking at, and then I realized she'd ask about Miles. Without him I don't know how long I would have stood staring at the starfish.

In the store, I bought an ice-cream cake and candles. I was debating taking Miles out of the house when I got back. For once, I'd tell him to come for a walk with his Dad. The starfish deserved at least two people to look at it, and I thought that with Miles was beside me, I'd be able to phone Nicola, and say, "Guess what I'm looking at?"

I was going slower on the way back. There were no small ice-cream cakes and it was an awkward thing to carry. The street was quiet with lights behind blinds and a stillness that made me more aware of the cold. Towards the end of the street, there was a house with a side-driveway and parked behind a pickup truck was a Mini.

I knew it was Nicola's before I saw the tiny shoe hanging from the rear-view mirror. It was the first shoe Miles had worn. I was hardly aware of the ice-cream cake I had in my hands or that I'd activated a motion light. When I realized, I felt exposed and ridiculous. There was a noise from the house and I jumped with the thought of Nicola appearing behind me.

Back on the street, I saw the house was number 15 and it was a split level.

"I'll be home late," she'd said, when she was leaving, "Don't wait up."

I didn't think of the dead starfish when I went by the beach the second time. I got into the house and put the ice-cream cake in the freezer and was afraid that I might get sick. I drank some water and felt the pain in my chest. Eventually, Miles came to me saying he was hungry. He looked sad or maybe that was my impression. He has Nicola's eyes. He asked if I was alright when he was eating his cereal. I still had my jacket on and he reminded me that boots were not allowed in the house. He didn't say that I had been staring at him, though I had been.

Miles went to bed and for once I didn't say, "Don't tell Mom how late you were up."

I wanted to lie on the bed beside him, but his bed was a single so there was no room. Besides, I'd never done that and I could imagine his discomfort. Still, I took my time leaving and he said, "Dad, are you okay?"

I sat at the kitchen table and opened a beer and then I opened another one. After my third, I thought about walking back to that house and knocking on the door. My head was a mess thinking of Nicola with someone else, but I couldn't leave Miles. He was a light sleeper and it would frighten him to wake to an empty house. And the truth was, I was afraid Nicola would answer the door to that house, or worse, appear behind the man who answered the door, and she'd show no shock or surprise. She'd just look at me like she did when I told her the plans for Miles' birthday party.

I was in bed when she came in. I felt her at the door of the bedroom. Miles still liked the hall light on and Nicola did too, but she'd throw something at me if I said she was afraid of the dark. She stood there for a long time. The light would have reached me on the bed. I wondered what would she was looking at, my stiffness, or my hair sticking out from the covers, maybe she knew I was awake. Then I thought-she must have smelled the beer. I never drank with only Miles in the house, and I thought she might have been irritated. I didn't know how to feel, though I knew I couldn't face her or hear what she had to say. Eventually, she came into the room. I felt her weight on the bed and heard her undress. She slid in beside me. After a few minutes, I heard her crying, and still I couldn't move.

The birthday party went without incident. The cold ushered into the house when the boys arrived. Outside was a crystal blue day. Every now and again, there would be a slight tremor from a plane flying overhead on its way to or from the city. The boys played video games, ate pizza, whined about the girl's cake, and then played more video games. Nicola livened up whenever some of the mothers came to collect their sons and she chatted in the kitchen. Otherwise, she was quiet and I would have thought she was observing how I was doing, if she didn't appear so distant. I couldn't tell her about seeing her car or about the starfish, though once the boys were gone, I suggested that the three of us should go for a walk.

"A walk? What's gotten into you?" Nicola said, but not in a joking manner, more dismayed and sad. "I thought it might be nice," I said.

She said she was too tired. I asked if work was busy. She looked at me in a way that made me want to hide, before she said. "You and Miles should go for a walk."

A few clouds floated in the darkening sky, and it was cold enough to see the fog of our breath. There was a small crowd on the beach and when we joined them, we saw the starfish wasn't alone. There were starfish, sea urchins and crabs of all sizes, but it was the huge starfish I kept staring at. In the evening light, it was a shocking sight. I was ashamed to think how excited I'd been to see it the previous night.

"They're all dead," the man beside us said.

Miles asked what happened to them. No-one answered. He grasped my hand. A woman arrived with her little girl and the little girl started to cry. The woman hushed her and brought her away. Everyone started to disperse then, as if all that time they'd been waiting for a signal to go. Miles and I didn't continue on our walk. The dead creatures had made us silent and morose. Miles asked again what was going on and I hated that I couldn't tell him.

The sea-creatures were on the news. Our beach was not the only one to have them wash up. They were victims of a cold spell. A three degree drop in sea temperature made them vulnerable to rough seas. They became dislodged by large waves and washed ashore all along the coast.

Nicola didn't want to walk down to the beach with me when I told her.

"It's too sad," she said.

I couldn't concentrate when she was gone to work. Miles was tired, and he started to watch a movie. He asked if I wanted to watch it with him, but it was impossible to sit still. I had to go back to number 15. I told Miles I wanted to check on the beach and he made a face like, 'why would you do that?'

The city lights shone on people who were walking slowly around the beach, hunched up and ghost-like, and the grey forms that lay lifeless by their feet. Someone down there was singing a lamenting chant and her voice caught on the sea breeze.

The pickup was in the same spot as the night before. I walked by the house and by the next two before turning around. I would have loved to sit on the pavement and wait until daybreak, because I didn't want to look at that driveway again; to see her car two days in a row would have been too much, but her car wasn't parked beside the pickup. The relief made my legs weak. For a few minutes, I couldn't move. I thought I saw a shadow by a window and I waited to see his face. It would have been easier to confront him than Nicola, but he didn't come out and I had to go home. There were still people on the beach and more than one voice rising upward.

That night, I was drifting to sleep when Nicola came home. Again, she slid into bed, but she didn't cry, and I was aware of every one of her breaths. In the morning, I let her rest and I walked Miles to school. She was still in bed when I came back. When she finally rose, she said it had been weird at work. Some of the residents heard about the sea creatures washed ashore and were upset. Nicola's favorite resident, an old lady called Kate, wondered why people weren't doing anything to help them. Nicola was leaning against the counter with her coffee and still in her robe. She watched me, until I said, "I don't think there's much we can do for them."

I didn't want to tell her about the people singing. The sound had been too sorrowful.

The creatures kept coming onto the shore. Some beaches were blocked off to the public and children were having nightmares about giant starfish, crabs, and sea-urchins. In some cases, there were seabirds in the mix and I wondered what had happened to them. Had they swooped down to be caught with the masses, like being trampled in a crowd?

Nicola phoned on her way to work. She said there was a guy on the beach shouting that it was the end of the world. I heard a thunderous voice behind hers and a blast of horns. She said traffic had stopped to listen to him and she was going to be late for work. "Don't bring Miles down, okay?"

I said I was sure that man wouldn't be allowed stay there. He'd be arrested for disorderly conduct.

She said, "Please, don't go there."

At midnight, when Miles was asleep, I walked out of the house. I could make out the sound of the sea, but there were no shouts. The town was eerily quiet and I didn't want to go back inside. I would have loved to walk until I was too tired to stand, but I couldn't. So I just stayed outside until my hands grew numb.

Nicola slept late again, and I dropped Miles to school and walked back by the house. I listened inside and heard nothing, before closing the door and walking to the beach. There were a couple of vans on the beach. It was starting to rain and there were a few people huddled up watching men in overalls. They were picking up the dead sea-creatures and bringing them to the vans and dumping them inside. The idea of a clean-up was alarming because that meant every day we were seeing new sea-creatures being washed up. The sea suddenly had a dull, lifeless energy. A man was standing beside me. He was balding and red-faced. He wore a jacket, but underneath I saw he had a white apron. There was a bakery up the road and a barber-shop. I couldn't remember which one he was.

"You ever wonder what happens to roadkill?" he said.

He looked at me and then gestured to a small man in overalls.

"Well, now you know." I was sure he was the baker. "They're the same guys who clean the roads, what a job."

The smell hit me then, or rather it had been seeping into me for the last few seconds, and now I was full of the salty decay. It hung on me, so I had to take a second shower.

Nicola was quiet throughout the day, and I got the impression she was avoiding me. Any time I went into the room she was in, she left. I spent hours staring at the computer screen trying to figure out what to say to her.

Miles didn't seem to notice anything amiss with us. During dinner, he talked about the strangest creatures that had washed up, one supposedly was a thirteen foot long squid, and another creature looked like a starfish but with bones. Nicola thought the boney starfish was ridiculous. Miles said we didn't know what was out there. He wanted to go to beach after dinner to check the creatures out.

Nicola said, "This isn't some game, those things are dying."

She apologized when Miles got upset and I told her it was scary enough for him as it was. I'd told no-one about the vans and the removal, though I couldn't stop wondering where those creatures were being brought to. In four days, I hadn't managed to finish that one sentence.

Miles was quiet when I took him to the beach. It was cold, but the day had brightened and the bluer sky made the grey forms on the beach more pitiful. A group of teenagers, one girl and two boys, were prodding a starfish with a stick. It was small and the color had not yet fully faded. The kids were curious, not cruel, yet every time the flesh of the star fish was touched by the stick I flinched. Finally, the girl said they should stop and she looked around. I saw her disappointment and wondered what they'd been looking for with their sticks.

Nicola was curled up in bed when we got back. She was crying again, and I sat on the bed beside her.

"Do you ever get lonely?" she said. "I do, I get lonely."

"I know," I said. She looked at me with her red-rimmed eyes and I wanted to know what was going on in her head, but I couldn't ask. When I held her hand, she didn't pull away, but she didn't hold me either. Eventually she drifted to sleep.

She was gone to work early the next morning. I'd wanted to get up with her and make coffee and be with her without talking about my thesis, or the patients that drove her mad. I'd wanted to sit and be quiet like the night before, but I slept through her alarm. She never made much noise. She'd grab her things and get dressed in the bathroom, and slip out. I woke to her absence.

I walked Miles to school and I tried to work, but I kept thinking of Nicola on the bed and me sitting beside her. I kept thinking I should have said something to her. I had no idea what it was, but I started to worry that the comfort I got from that time together was completely one-sided. It was impossible to concentrate. The apartment felt too small and without Nicola, I was aware of every sound. I had never noticed before the heat ticking in the walls, the whirring noise of the light, or the slight buzzing from the computer. Now the sounds grated my senses and all I wanted was for her to come home.

I had to walk, but I didn't go near the beach. I went towards Miles' school and took turns that would keep me away from the sea creatures in case I might hear their sound, a low dying moan maybe, or the scuttle of their bodies on the sand.

It was Friday—I hadn't realized the day, which wasn't unusual. Miles frowned when he saw me waiting at the school. Apparently he had a sleepover planned. This wouldn't have annoyed me before, but now I asked why no one told me. Miles shrugged and said he didn't think he had to.

He said, "Dad, I have to go."

Back at the house, I put on the radio and put the volume on high. The DJ's voices irritated me, but I didn't think of putting on other music. I had two beers by the time Nicola came home, and I'd called the local restaurant to make a reservation. She stalled inside the door. Nicola is a small woman with a pretty face and serious probing eyes. She was regarding me with some surprise, but there was an element of impatience when I told her I'd booked a table.

"We haven't been out in ages," I said.

A plane flew overhead sending tremors through the house and adding the sensation of distance between us. I expected her to argue, but she nodded and said okay.

It was quicker to get to the restaurant by turning left from the house and walking by the beach, but I didn't want to go that way. I thought I heard chanting come from there, though Nicola said she didn't hear anything. She didn't complain when I said we should walk the long way around. I wondered if she'd seen the sea creatures on her way to and from work, if they'd had the same effect on her as they did me, but I didn't want to ask about them. Instead I asked how her day was.

She said, "Is that what you want to ask? How my day was?"

Clouds hung low in the sky. There was a flashing light moving towards the city and I said yes without looking at her.

"My day was fine," she said.

The restaurant was Italian, and had white table clothes, dim lights and a sea view that we declined. Across the road, there was no beach. The waves came as far as the rocks and spilled over them. Any sea creatures would have been bashed against them. The thought made me want to leave, and I might have only Nicola was already following the waiter to the back of the restaurant and a table for two. The place was empty bar us. "It's quiet," I said to the waiter and he nodded and told us that business was down because of what was happening on the beach. People didn't want to go out, while that was going on, and it wasn't only the sea creatures, but the people they attracted. His face scrunched up when he said this. Nicola agreed with him and said she'd heard the screams of Armageddon. While I thought of the kids I'd seen poking at the sea creatures and the hope on their faces.

I said, "It's sad."

The waiter shrugged. He said, "There's no seafood."

Nicola laughed. He said. "Seriously, there were a lot of angry people asking how we could serve seafood when they were dying on the beach."

Nicola glanced at me cnd I wanted to react, to laugh or say how ridiculous it was, but a part of me agreed.

We ordered a bottle of wine. I heard the mumble of the

waiter, and then his steps on the floor coming back to us and the pop of the wine, and I had no idea how to fill the spaces in between. None of the dishes looked appealing to me.

Nicola was looking at the menu when she said, "I saw you outside the house."

My heart stopped. I stared at the top of Nicola's head waiting for her to look at me, but she kept studying her menu. Finally, she put it beside her and entwined her fingers in a way I'd often seen her gran doing, only with Nicola, there had always been a shy seductiveness with the gesture when she'd place her chin on those hands and gaze over at me. Now, with her elbows on the table, she put her cheek on her hands and looked towards the window and the sea.

I asked, "Who is he?"

I thought she might say that I didn't want to know. But she said his name was Paul. She said, "You don't know him."

"How do you know him?"

"Is that important?"

My glass of wine was gone and my head was spinning. The waiter came and she told him her order. I thought if I reached out, I wouldn't be able to touch her. She was so far away. I ordered meatballs because it was the only dish I could think of.

With the waiter gone, she sat back loose in her chair; all these poses I knew from our years together, though I couldn't read them now. Her face was softer than it had been and I didn't like that it might have been because she'd spoken his name; maybe he was the reason for her sitting in that coy way of hers. I noticed her fingernails were painted a light pink when she reached for her wine. I said I was sorry, and she paused and looked at me. Some of her tenderness had faded.

She didn't ask what I was sorry for. I couldn't tell her it was because I hadn't noticed her nails before or how tired she looked.

She said, "After I saw you, I didn't know if I should go home, but I couldn't stay away. I expected you to be waiting for me. I thought you'd be angry and demand answers, that you'd do something."

I told her I was afraid to say something and give her an opening to leave, and it sounded stupid to think she needed an opening from me.

I said, "I didn't know what to say to you."

"No, you never do," she said.

The waiter was coming with our food, and I had to look away from Nicola. I poured wine and once the waiter was gone, I told her that she wasn't the best at fucking talking either. She could have come to me if she was lonely. She could have told me before falling into bed with the first guy who came along.

She was staring at me, and I fell back in the chair. I realized what she was going to say seconds before she said it.

At home, she threw her coat over the couch and went straight for the bathroom. I heard the water run and knew she'd be in there for an hour at least. I hadn't eaten much, and the glasses of wine made me feel lightheaded. I wished I hadn't had them or the beers earlier so I'd have had a clearer head when my wife said, "I did try to tell you."

We'd walked home in silence. With her, I felt tongue-tied and awkward. I had no idea what to say—I'm sorry hadn't been enough the first or second time. Across the table from me, she'd nodded and said, "So, am I."

The water stopped running. The house ticked with life. I leaned against the doorway and asked, "Do you love him?"

She didn't answer. I imagined her lying in the bath with her body submerged in water, and her eyes closed. I sat on the ground and started talking. I told her about wanting to go back to his house to get her, and being afraid that she would refuse to come; about my urge to lie down with Miles and regret that I couldn't, because I'd never done it. I told her now we spent time together. I told her about being awake and hearing her cry, about my visits to the house to see if she was there and how hard it was anytime she left. I told her that I missed her and I don't know what else I said. I just kept talking until she opened the door with her face red from the steam and then I watched her walk to the bedroom and waited until I knew she was lying down before following her.

The next morning, I heard Nicola get up and get ready. I waited to see if she might come in and say goodbye, but she didn't. She never said if she loved him either. The night before, the two of us had lain stiff on the bed for a long time before finally falling asleep. She might have been waiting for me to ask that question again, but once was enough.

She worked every second Saturday and it was a short

shift ending at 2 p.m. Miles wasn't coming home until the evening, but it was impossible to get work done. Eventually, I couldn't stand being away from her a moment longer.

While I waited for the bus that would bring me close to the nursing home where she worked, I saw there were more sea creatures. The waves were washing over them and I saw what looked like a sea urchin being dragged onto the sand.

When the bus came, I nearly didn't get on. I almost ran down to the beach to join the other people wandering around. The crowd was walking slowly, as if they were being pulled down by the great weight on the sand.

The residential home wasn't too far from our apartment. During the summer months, Nicola could cycle, and I could have the car to take Miles wherever he had to go. I'd waited to get the bus, until she only had a half hour to work.

The residential home was a large two-story building with a small garden in front and a driveway at the side with a car-park for the employees. The driveway led to the back garden, which had a path along the edges and some benches. Once, when I walked up with Miles, we waited for Nicola in that garden and the silence surprised me.

I saw them the moment I turned towards the driveway. She had her back to me and was shaking her head. Her hand was by her face and he went to touch her arm. She pulled away and then looked at me. He must have followed her gaze. Then he probably stopped talking and stared at where I stood, but I wasn't watching him. I was watching my wife who turned towards me and whose eyes widened. Her mouth fell open. For the first time since seeing her car outside his house, I wanted to cry.

The man said something and she shook her head again. She didn't look at him and I imagined them staring out at me, while I stood by her car that first night. Nicola started to fumble for her car keys. She said something to the man and glanced at me before walking to the car. I followed her and the silence of the place wore on me. At the car, I asked if I should drive and I refused to look at where he'd been standing. She didn't look at me when she nodded and handed me the keys. In the car, she folded down in the seat and looked as if she wanted to disappear. Once on the street, I put on the radio to ease the quiet and she turned it off.

I felt her gaze on my face, but she turned away when I looked at her.

I said, "So that's how you know him?"

I didn't expect an answer but she mumbled yes.

When we were near the beach, she sat straighter and wiped her eyes. The kids I'd seen that night with Miles were there. I saw the girl running toward the sea with what looked like a sea urchin. There were others with them and everyone was running fast.

"What are you doing?" Nicola said, when I stopped the car.

"I don't fucking know," I said. "We should do something though."

I think she smiled then. At least that's how I remember it.

"Come on," I said.

For a moment, I was afraid that she'd say no, she wasn't

going, but then there was a nod, and the two of us were out of the car, running towards the beach.

The girl saw us coming and she said, "Some of them are alive."

"This one," an older woman shouted, and I ran to help her carry the starfish out to sea.

Confession

Nollaig Sheehy sat two seats from the front pew with her coat fastened. Her hands were folded on her knees. The priest's late start didn't concern her, as he was probably called out to an ailing parishioner. A few children were restless. She heard the whimpers and the hushing noises of mothers. But mostly the congregation waited with nothing more than the occasional whisper and shuffle. When the priest appeared red-cheeked and breathless in his white linen vestment, Nollaig was thinking of the roast beef she would cook for herself and Margaret.

Father Divine, a young priest, with a thick head of dark hair, grasped the side of the pulpit and leaned forward to tell the congregation that a terrible thing had happened.

"Nick Moody was grievously hurt," the priest said. "He was bludgeoned and found behind the Dun Maeve Pub."

Nollaig thought he was looking directly at her. She was

convinced she'd missed his last words, and he'd said something about her daughter, Margaret Sheehy, who had been working in the Dun Maeve last night.

Fr. Divine was speaking about the community helping one another in this time of need, and Nollaig was thinking of her daughter standing by the back door of the pub. No matter the weather, she liked to go out there so she could hear the rush of the river beside her.

Nollaig realized she was standing. Her head was light. She could feel the people's attention move over her and the worry that had risen from her movement. Many present must have realized that Margaret had been working last night. There was a collective intake of breath. Neighbor knees tilted sideways. Nollaig stumbled into the aisle.

The priest's voice followed her out of the church, but she heard nothing of the words. Last night's rain had brought out the dark hues of the countryside. The road was quiet. Nollaig weaved through the cars parked in front. Somewhere close a dog was barking and she imagined Margaret hurt, or still hiding in the pub.

Nollaig's breathing felt trapped inside her head. She ran, then walked, then ran again. She took the short cut through the primary school, silent now on Sunday with the quarry closed and beyond it the sea was a rolling grey mass towards the bay. Clouds drifted above her and there was tightness in her chest.

It took three efforts to get her key in the front door latch. Nollaig didn't bother taking it out. In her hurry, she left the front door open. Her daughter's room was at the front of the bungalow. Nollaig opened the door to darkness and a scent of unwashed clothes. Her daughter's form was huddled under the covers in bed. Nollaig turned on the light to reveal her daughter's dark hair and pale skin.

"Hey!" Margaret said, "Turn the light off."

Nollaig couldn't move. Her daughter was rising in the bed, and Nollaig was looking at the wet clothes that had been thrown on the floor.

"Mammy, what is it?" Margaret said.

For a moment, Nollaig couldn't speak.

"Mammy," Margaret urged, and the worry in her voice pulled Nollaig back. She told her, "Nick Moody was hurt last night."

"What do you mean hurt? What happened?" Margaret said.

Nollaig was shaking her head. She said she didn't know. She said she'd run home as soon as she heard, because she was so worried. "You get up, I'll put the kettle on," she said.

Nollaig was standing by her kitchen window when she saw the Garda car drive into the estate and towards them.

Across from Margaret, was a female detective with short blonde hair, thoughtful navy eyes, a slim figure and wrists that looked small enough to break with touch. She had introduced herself as Hennessy. Her partner sat beside her. McMahon was his name. He had broad shoulders and pale green eyes over a small nose and thin mouth. There was some grey in his hair, though his face was young.

In her pajamas, Margaret looked like a large child beside them.

"I didn't go out the back. I was going to," Margaret said, "but the rain sounded awful." She paused and shook her head. "I left the bin bag by the back door."

Nollaig felt numb, as if she were watching this scene from afar. It was too much to think of her daughter standing at that back door, her hand on the handle, the absurdity of it all. McMahon asked if Nick Moody left with anyone.

"No," Margaret said, "He left alone just after 11 p.m."

The last customer was gone by 1 a.m. Margaret had finished cleaning and had gone out the front. She said she'd gotten soaked running to her mother's car. She'd driven because the forecast warned of rain, and she didn't like walking alone at that hour anyway, no matter how short the journey. She saw no one on her way home.

"Did anything unusual happen last night, any arguments?" Hennessy asked.

Nollaig had to fight the urge to run to her daughter and tell her not to say anything more. The seconds of silence pulled at her and made the swish of the washing machine sound loud and oppressive. She had not looked at her daughter's clothes when she'd grabbed them from the floor. They were the only things in the washing machine now, one pair of pants with socks and a black shirt.

Margaret said no, nothing strange happened.

"Are you sure?" Hennessy asked.

Margaret had a habit of biting her lip when concentrating. As a child, she used to chew her hair. After a while, she said, "Yes, I'm sure, nothing happened."

A glance out the kitchen window showed the day had turned darker. Clouds crowded the sky. Nollaig wanted to be on the other side of the glass, far away from here. The room was stuffy and hot. Hennessy asked who Nick was with last night.

Margaret said, "His wife Joan, but she didn't stay long."

She said she couldn't imagine how she was now. A silence reigned after this, and Nollaig wondered if her daughter was waiting for news, if she expected the police to lean forward and tell her something of the wife. Hennessy glanced at her partner with the mention of the wife's name. Nollaig was sure they had been the bearers of bad news; the two had stood at Joan's door. Maybe Hennessy had held the wife up after the shock.

Hennessy said, "Who else was there?"

Margaret recited a list of names, including their neighbor Raymond.

McMahon scribbled the names down. Nollaig wondered what the Garda would learn about Margaret. They would probably talk to Raymond, since he was in the pub. She could imagine them at his kitchen table, huddled as they were now. It was possible Raymond would remember spending time with Margaret when they were children. Margaret was never happy watching him. There were one or two instances where Nollaig found Raymond close to crying.

Would the detectives learn that Margaret had no friends and a sketchy employment record? Before the pub, she'd worked in a clothes shop in Sligo town. The manager, a forty-ish, well-kept woman with blonde hair and judicious eye had agreed to take Margaret on part-time. Within the first week, Margaret had come home telling Nollaig that she had dressed the window and had been asked to order the clothes for next week. Nollaig had sat at the kitchen table, listening with a sinking sensation in her gut. Days before Margaret had stopped going to work; their dinners had been eaten quietly. Margaret had stopped grabbing her mother's arm and saying, "Wait till I tell you." Nollaig had been foolish enough to feel relieved with the end of the lies. She should have known her daughter had had her fun and was getting bored. It had happened with the courses in hairdressing and computers she'd started with a flourish, then let fizzle out. Still, it had been a shock when Margaret announced she wasn't going into the shop. By the time the owner of the pub asked if Margaret wanted to work a few shifts, she'd been unemployed six months.

Nollaig hadn't heard the last questions asked. The voices rose and fell and she wondered if the detectives were aware of sounds of washing machine that rumbled by the sink. Nollaig shook with the worry that she'd forgotten to pour detergent in before turning the machine on. The Garda had gotten out of the car by then and were walking towards the house. Margaret had stalled in the hall when she saw them. She'd looked frightened.

"It'll be okay," Nollaig had told her on her way to the door.

A scrape of the chair brought Nollaig's attention back to the table. McMahon and Hennessy were standing.

"Let us know if you think of anything else?" Hennessy said and Nollaig noticed the white card that had been placed on the table as she walked them out.

"It's a shock," McMahon said to Nollaig, and she realized how pale she must look, how shaken and disheveled. She had lost the power of speech. 'I know,' she wanted to say, but there was nothing in her mouth.

From the door, she watched them drive away. When she went back to the kitchen, her daughter turned to look at her.

Margaret's eyes were red but focused. "Isn't it terrible Mammy?" she said.

Nollaig couldn't answer. Her tongue felt too heavy in her mouth. She didn't know how she was standing.

The house was narrow and painted a light pink color. There was one window to the right of the front door with wooden blinds. It looked innocent, tucked between two nondescript buildings, and a few yards from the train station Margaret had to walk to and from every day. She'd passed the house seventeen times before she noticed the bronze plaque, and paused to read it. The words surprised her, but not as much as they might have eight months ago, when she'd imagined the seediest thing she'd ever have to contend with were the roaming eyes of the drunks she served at the local pub, and how they'd call her over with a quick movement of their head. She'd have to lean forward to hear their order, feel their beer-sodden breath on her cheek. Through the side window, she saw there was nothing innocent about that room with the armchairs hidden behind the door, so the men waiting would have the benefit of seeing the ladies enter from behind. But there was nothing innocent about Margaret either. That's why she left home and flew to the other side of the world. She could have gone to the States. She had relatives there, but she'd wanted to go where no one knew her, where she could start from scratch and build herself up into someone different. Her eyes met the reflection in the sun-splashed window. Dark hair, heavy-boned, big-eyed, loose of shoulder, she moved on.

Margaret had been staying in a hostel up the road and living out of her suitcase since she'd arrived in the country. For the last months at home, while she'd waited for her visa to come through, she'd hardly left her bedroom. Days were slept away, and nights were spent watching movies on the small portable TV she'd bought when her mother's silent existence started to get on her nerves.

After Nick Moody's death, little could be said about her behavior or her need to stay safe inside. She'd ignored calls from her peers who lived close-by. They'd phoned because their parents said they should. Margaret needed some sup-port, a shoulder to lean on. She knew the calls had been their parents' idea because they'd stopped there. No-one bothered to come to her front door. Margaret had imagined the neigh-bors shaking heads and whispering that it must have been shocking to realize there had been an attack only a few feet away. They would have thought about Margaret alone and vulnerable in the pub; a few might have imagined what would have happened, if she'd stepped out to the back of pub, like she normally did.

"No wonder she hasn't gone back," they would have said. "It's a shock."

Whenever she'd ventured out of the house, the pity in their eyes made her go cold. There was no curiosity about her being the only one in the pub when it happened—Margaret Sheehy, the big quiet girl with the pretty eyes.

If it had been Louise, they'd have wondered why he was at the back of the pub in the first place. They would have looked at Louise's slim figure and blonde hair and come up with a different answer.

But it wasn't Louise, who liked to flirt behind the counter. It was Margaret who on her first night tending bar couldn't talk. Their questions were smiled at and left unanswered until the customers gave up.

The hostel was quiet just after 2 p.m. Margaret's shift in the café finished at noon. She used to hate this time of day. Now she got through listless afternoons by napping. She could sleep until five if her roommate, an English girl who spent most of her time on the roof smoking, didn't come in to rummage through her rucksack. Then Margaret would walk around the city for hours. She went all the way to Bondi once. She'd lost weight since she got here, but could do nothing about those big thigh bones.

Her hostel room smelt of sweat and beer, the English

girl's input, and grease, which was Margaret's. The café she worked in was a busy fast-food place and suited her perfectly. From the moment she entered at 6 a.m., she was kept busy; preparing food, serving customers, and cleaning their mess. The owners didn't keep her a minute past needing her. She got her lunch when she finished and ate on the high counter by the window.

The air was hot and muggy, but this never bothered Margaret. Nights, she tossed and turned with flashes of skin and blood. The feel of cold stone against her palm would wake her more than once, and she'd jump breathless from the bed, expecting to see the bloodied stone before her, as if it was possible that it had been unearthed from the bottom of the river and could find her oceans away.

The afternoon sun, though hot and intrusive, kept the dreams back and let her drift to sleep unhindered. Only not today, because today she couldn't stop thinking of the bronze sign and the women behind it—and this made her think of the parish priest at home. Hidden behind the red curtain with his face made up of tiny squares from the screen that divided him and his confessors, the quiet man became someone different every Saturday evening. He was the voice of power, as with a flattened hand he made the figure of the cross and gave penance. He never looked you in the eye, so Margaret believed he couldn't help feeling a little ashamed by the sins he was made to hear.

One Our Father and three Hail Mary's was his usual. How much would he have given her?

Her knees would have been raw by the end of it, even if

he understood, even if he knew she had no choice, because that's the way she would have told it. She'd lied too many times to stop now.

The Guards had come to Margaret's house to interview her a second time. They'd apologized for making her think of that night, but they needed to make sure she hadn't seen anyone linger. She'd started crying when one of them, a young red-cheeked man with watery eyes, said the violence against Nick Moody had to have been personal. When she looked at him wide-eyed and swore she saw no one, he'd apologized for upsetting her.

She'd heard the rumors about an affair with a woman who lived on Station Road. She was separated over a year and the Guards had been at her house several times, though it was hard to imagine how the whispers had reached Margaret behind the closed door of her bedroom. She might have heard some murmur of it the day she gave her notice in the pub. Margaret knew the wife had been more angry than hurt. With her two young children asleep upstairs, she'd told Guards it was probably some jealous husband. Everyone had known the deceased to wait in the dark for someone else's wife.

Still, no one thought that he might have waited for Margaret. Maybe, that's why she decided to leave, because at home she was so easy to overlook. When she applied for the visa and booked the ticket, she thought she was saying goodbye to the notion that she was the type of woman nothing ever happened to. This idea seemed to follow her, and each time Margaret passed the building with its bronze plaque; the deceit of its pink childlike exterior pulled at her and made her want to expose what lay underneath.

Six days after reading the plaque, she couldn't sleep. The English girl had moved out and Margaret was surprised by her loneliness. She dressed in a long black skirt and t-shirt, and went to the small shop tucked in front of the train station to buy a pencil and writing pad. She looked through the newspapers and jotted down the title of the one she'd say she worked for. "I'd like to interview the girls," she'd say, when it wouldn't be about them at all.

The front door to the parlor was opened by a slim brunette woman dressed in a pink business suit. She looked like a doll with her shiny complexion and small wrists and ankles. Her hair fell thick on her shoulders and her narrow eyes moved up and down Margaret in a way that made her feel naked. She wasn't entirely sure if she disliked the sensation.

"I'd like to interview the girls for an article," Margaret said.

"Really?" the brunette answered.

Margaret tried to say yes. The name of the paper she'd picked was on her tongue but she couldn't let it fall. There was something about the woman that suggested she saw right through Margaret. The woman looked amused, though there was a hard glimmer in her eyes that made that amusement less personal.

"You can talk to Taylor. Are you thinking of trying it?"

Margaret wasn't sure what the woman meant, but she nodded and stepped inside. The walls were painted a color between pink and red, a warm color that made Margaret feel claustrophobic. The floor had a brown carpet. A smell of perfume was stronger at the foot of the stairs than anywhere else and made Margaret think of ghosts, or that some of the girls' spirit lingered at the spot. Her gaze slipped quickly away from the stairs that fell into the hall, as if it was something perverse. She watched the gentle sway of the woman's hips, as she led the way to a small cluttered room at the back of the house. The room resembled a living room with its couch and two chairs. Clothes were strung over the back of the couch, and a bag of makeup was on the coffee table, its contents spilled outward. The window to the left of the door looked out to a concrete yard, and a girl with messy, dyed red hair, dressed in a short shirt and vest top, sat below the beams of sunlight that reached over her head. She could have been any age from fifteen to twenty-five. She had a small compact body that exuded energy.

"This is Taylor," the brunette said, and looked at Margaret in the appraising way she'd seen men look at Louise. "Sorry. I didn't get your name".

"Margaret."

"Is that your real name?"

Margaret nodded.

The woman smiled, "Yeah. I thought so."

She said Taylor would tell her everything she needed to know. Taylor was too small, too young, too full of life, so Margaret listened, and wouldn't have said anything about herself even if she got the chance. Once Taylor started talking, there was no stopping her. Margaret was awed by the rapid movement of Taylor's thin painted lips as she talked about moving from Queensland with her father, after she'd spent years in the wrong company. She'd started young. At the tender age of fourteen, she had sex in the back of a car and was paid with crumpled bills. Taylor's father tried to keep her on the straight and narrow, but there were too many windows to watch and too many people waiting on corners. Finally, he packed his family up and moved across the sprawling Country, putting the desert between his daughter and the people she'd met.

Taylor worked in a laundromat for a couple of weeks and a café for three days, but she couldn't stand the idea of putting in so many hours for measly pay when in Queensland she made a few hundred in a day. When she paused, Margaret thought the small parting of her lips looked like a full stop.

It was early afternoon. There was only one other girl who was busy in one of the rooms upstairs. After a half an hour, and most of Taylor's life story, the doorbell signaled the end of their conversation. Margaret had to wait until the man was brought upstairs before she could leave. Walking back through that narrow corridor, she felt too much like the priest, seeing only the patterns people wanted her to see, and showing nothing of herself.

"Can I come tomorrow?" She asked.

The brunette shrugged, "You could try it out, see if you like it".

She smiled. "Girls will get fed up talking. You'll have to make up your mind soon."

Margaret nodded and felt a tingling of surprise. She wasn't sure if she should feel flattered or not.

"And you'll have to think of a better name."

The next day, Margaret was led into the small courtyard that was surrounded by high stone walls. The sky appeared close enough to touch. A young woman in a short black dress with thin shoulders straps was sitting at the only table. Her legs were stretched before her and her high heels were slipping off slender feet. A cigarette burned in the full ashtray beside her. The brunette introduced the woman as Sam.

"And this is Margaret. She wants to ask you a few questions," she said and retreated with sharp clicks of her heels.

Sam took a cigarette from her pack and lit it. With the pull of her cigarette, her cheeks were drawn in to make her look skeletal. Smoke rose above her rouged cheeks and heavily painted eye lids. Her brown lipstick was thick and smudged. Margaret imagined this carelessness might have been sexy to some of the men who came. It hinted at a kind of risquéness. To Margaret, it made Sam look as if she had been playing dress up and the game had gone on too long. The borders and boundaries erased themselves, so the girl hadn't known when to stop, and that was why the woman ended up in this courtyard, in the middle of a city, waiting for a doorbell to ring.

Margaret told her she was interviewing all the girls for an article. The masseuse smiled. Margaret expected her to ask about the paper she worked for, as Taylor had done. The excitement in her eyes had dimmed with 'The Herald' as if she had hoped for better. Sam's lack of curiosity made Margaret feel transparent. A line of sweat tickled her upper lip, and she resisted the urge to wipe it. The gesture would have reminded her of how Nick Moody had wiped the white foam of Guinness from his lips.

"So, what do you want to know?" Sam asked. Her thumb and pointer fingers had thick silver rings. Her humorless gaze pulled at the nerves in Margaret's stomach.

"I talked to Taylor yesterday," she said.

Sam was looking at Margaret, as if nothing about her visitor might interest her, as if she knew everything there was to know because she was big-boned and plain.

"Yeah?" she said between drags of her cigarette.

"Yes," Margaret's mouth had gone dry. The belief that she could be honest with these women dissolved at her feet and made her want to cry. She went towards the empty chair and tried to ignore the muscles of Sam's calves. Margaret imagined Taylor and Sam talking about her. They probably laughed at the thought of the frumpy girl working here or having to see her dressed in skimpy clothes.

Sam's fringe came down over one eye. She leaned forward to tap ash into the crowded ash-tray. "Taylor lied to you. Her dad didn't bring her to Sydney."

Margaret remembered the red hair lying loose around Taylor's neck, her vest top clinging to her flat boy-like breasts, her short bare legs, and the glint in her blue eyes.

"Taylor followed her pimp. He says he loves her, but wasn't happy with the deduction in funds when she started to go straight. He brought her here."

Sam looked Margaret over, smiling at her dress with its long sleeves and the lack of naked skin.

"Taylor thought you'd follow your dad before a lover."

Margaret couldn't answer. Her nerves had flattened and hardened inside her and made her so angry at this young woman with the smooth skin and self-assurance. Sam knew what it was like to pretend, and yet she looked at Margaret and came up with the same conclusion as those fools on the other side of the world.

Sam tipped her ash into the ashtray, and Margaret felt the same irritation when she opened the back door of the pub and realized he was there. She hadn't been scared, which surprised her. Instead there was a kind of relief in having something she could fight against. Sam took a long drag from her cigarette, and Margaret remembered him stepping from the shadows and the sound of the river hitting against the wall behind them. He'd smelt of beer and cigarettes and she'd hit him with the first thing she could find.

"I didn't have to kill him," Margaret said, and felt the instant change in the air. She thought Sam was finding it hard to breathe. "He was lying on the ground, and I dropped the rock on his face. Then I threw it in the water and finished cleaning the bar as if nothing happened. I drove home and went to bed and didn't even think of him."

Margaret smiled and after a drawn-out silence that made her sit straighter, she said, "I'd follow a lover. I wouldn't let him tell me what to do though."

Sam's lips had parted and Margaret thought again that

Sam looked like a child caught in the middle of dress up. The clock ticked in the make shift living-room and there was a distant sound of traffic. A cloud skimmed by unnoticed. Margaret was in no rush to leave. The woman sitting before her had dropped her gaze. She said nothing, but Margaret heard her apology in the silence. It would have sounded something like his; a pleading tone in the voice. The bell rang and still Margaret didn't move. She waited for the brunette to come back and then Margaret rose.

"I'm done here," she said, and the woman looked at Sam who had deflated in her seat. Then she looked at Margaret as if she had no idea what she was.

Taking Too Many Chances

The new house was narrow with a small patch of green in the back and nothing but the street in the front. Eva could not get used to the lack of space and how dark the kitchen was by the afternoon. She hated that when she left her house there was the possibility of running into her neighbors. To her left was a young couple who looked very much alike. To her right, was an elderly man who unnerved her with his habit of staring whenever she walked her children to the school bus. Ten-year-old Mason walked in front of her and refused to answer when she called, and six-year-old Lucy complained about having to hold her hand.

In her other house with the large windows, Eva used to drive her children to school. She used to bring them to their after-school activities and sit with the other moms, and sense their curiosity because she was younger than most. She was only twenty-two when Mason was born, nineteen, when

Charlie sat at one of her tables she'd waitressed and gave her a card that said McManus construction. "It's my father's business," he'd said, and she'd thought his statement modest.

Now, five mornings a week, Eva drove to the insurance office on Main Street where she answered the phone and listened to her colleague Izzy rant about one of her many cats. Their cubicles were side-by-side and in the eight weeks Eva worked there, she'd heard about the cat that disappeared for a month and had woken Izzy in the middle of the night by scratching her front door. There was also the cat that had lost an eye. It had been in Izzy's apartment all day so she had no idea how the eye was lost or where it had gone to and it still gave her the shivers. That story sickened Eva too, and she found the cat that acted like a dog, running to the door and hissing at visitors, disturbing. Izzy told these stories over the wall of the cubicle with her round face scrunched up. She'd pause now and again for Eva to say little more than, "Oh wow," or "Gosh," because Eva was trying not to show her Boston accent after the first day when Izzy said, "You're from Boston, aren't you?"

Eva said no, and felt tense with the expectation of questions, and having to describe her life up to now. She would have preferred to forget the apartment in Boston and coming home to find her mother on the floor in the kitchen, and all the subsequent places that led her to the restaurant where Charlie arrived one evening. For a long time, she had forgotten that apartment and all those places before meeting Charlie, until he came home from work and stood in the bright kitchen and said, "I hear South Carolina is nice."

"Nice for what?" Eva said.

She was sitting at the wide counter looking for a recipe for dinner. She was smiling until she noticed the worried expression on his face. When he'd started talking, she felt as she did when she'd closed the door of that apartment and heard the water in the kitchen running and received no greeting from her mother.

"I thought you'd gone on holidays?" Izzy said.

She always heard Eva come in. Eva had barely sat down before Izzy was watching her with child-like awe, which was strange to behold on a middle-aged woman. Sometimes, it made Eva feel good or superior or both and she liked the feeling, which was probably why she'd told Izzy in a moment of weakness that they owned the apartment they were going to on Marco Island.

"No, tomorrow," Eva said.

Charlie had been counting down the days since his boss offered him the place for a week after some favor or other.

"Three more days' kids," he'd say, and wink.

Mason would say, "Yeah Dad."

Lucy would clap, and Eva would just about manage not to roll her eyes at her husband because Mason would be watching her.

Alone, she'd tell Charlie to stop acting like a kid. He would tell her that he was not acting. He'd stopped winking at her since she'd thrown her boot at him and said he had no right to that anymore. But he still tried putting his arm around her and she'd squirm away from him, not caring about his hurt and confusion.

"Are you still driving there?" Izzy said.

They'd gone through this twice before. Izzy hated driving, or she would have if she'd ever learned, but she hadn't, because she didn't trust people. For her, it was insane to get into a metal box and share the road with people you didn't know, especially when it was for nine hours. Eva refused to look at her and said, "I need to get this done."

Izzy might have nodded. She definitely lingered with her fingers over the flimsy wall. Her nails were painted a sickening orange. Eventually, Eva swiveled in the chair and asked, "What is it?"

"I have a bad feeling about it," Izzy said, "Something's going to happen and it's not good."

Eva imagined throwing the pen so it would hit Izzy right between the eyes. Instead, she breathed deeply, a trick she'd learned at eighteen when she first went to live with her aunt and uncle, and said, "Okay, we'll fly."

Izzy gushed, "Really?"

In her head, Eva was screaming, but she said, "Absolutely, of course."

Her voice remained light and carefree with the slight English tone, which made Izzy curious. To her questions of 'where are you from?', she'd only gotten, "Around" or "Mostly all over."

"We have to fly to Marco," Eva told Charlie during dinner.

He paused with the fork of spaghetti near his mouth,

and she saw the worry because they could not afford to fly. If his boss hadn't given them his place, they would not be able to go on a holiday. Eva imagined Charlie going to the boss and wringing his hands, saying he needed to do something to cheer his wife up. Maybe he talked about how sad and angry she was, and the boss said, "A holiday is what she needs." Either version appalled her.

"Why?" he asked, and she told him Izzy had a bad feeling about the drive.

"Lucky she's not driving then."

Little Lucy's eyes had widened. "What bad feeling?"

Mason said he didn't want to fly. He hated flying. Eva patted Lucy's hand, and said it was okay, because Izzy's crazy. Charlie laughed at this. Eva wasn't laughing. She was telling the truth.

"But you said we had to fly," Lucy said.

Eva said, "Never mind. I was only joking."

Mason said again that he hated flying. Eva snapped and asked how he could hate flying when he hadn't flown since he was a baby. They used to vacation at their house in Kennebunk and they didn't have to fly there. The glance Mason threw at Charlie enraged her further. She said, "You need to think for yourself."

"He doesn't want to fly," Charlie said. "That's thinking for himself."

"He doesn't want to fly because you don't want to fly."

"I can't afford to fly. I would if I could, but he doesn't want to. It's entirely different"

"Jesus Christ," Eva said.

She couldn't stand being in the same room as her husband, since his father had a stroke and Charlie came home from work and said the business had no money, at least none that was theirs.

Charlie didn't call her back this time. In her bedroom, she could hear the tinkle of the knives and forks and hated that the house was so small, but it was the laughter that made her cry.

"Kids have short memories," Charlie said when he sat on the bed beside her. She cried silently, so it was possible he didn't know. She held her breath, waiting for him to continue and finish the thought, but he sat still and quiet for several seconds. Then he rose and left the room.

By 6 a.m. the next day, Lucy and Mason were in the car in their pajamas with a blanket over them. Charlie had set up a computer for the kids so they could watch a movie later and he'd packed a lunch. Eva's sorrow lingered. She was aware of it, like it was a lump in her seat. For the first few hours, the children slept. Then, they stopped at a rest stop with picnic tables outside. The squat building had maps on the walls and bathrooms where the children changed. Above them was a clear blue sky. Eva wanted to stay in that rest stop, or to turn around and give back the key to the boss and say 'no thanks we don't need your help'. When the others started to cleanup, she searched for the brilliant red of a Cardinal in the trees, because Mason told her that they were the state bird of North Carolina.

"Are you coming?" Charlie said, with the driver's door opened. His arms were resting on the roof of the car, and a glance at her children in the back seat shoving each other kept Eva quiet.

When they'd first told the kids they were moving, Mason had looked up North Carolina and had come running down to Eva in the kitchen to tell her that North Carolina was the best place to live in the U.S.

"Isn't that great?" he'd said.

Lucy had cried, because she had to leave her best friend Emily.

"Georgia has the biggest peaches in the world," Mason said now. "Maybe we'll see one."

Charlie laughed and said, "I think that's peach farms Mason, not peaches."

"Yeah that's what I said and it's famous for peanuts."

When they grew tired of looking for peach and peanut farms, they played a game of 'I Spy' until they got bored. The kids watched a movie. Lucy felt sick, but she didn't vomit. Mason got impatient in their seventh hour and asked if they were there yet so many times Charlie snapped and said 'that was enough'. Eva sunk in her seat and thought maybe Izzy was right.

They arrived at the apartment building at 7p.m. exhausted, ragged and bad-tempered. The children cheered up when they entered the lobby with the thick carpet and leather couches and mirrors on the walls. Mason went straight to the doors on the left which led to a gym and a games room. "There's a pool table Dad."

"There's a swimming pool too, but it's too late to go looking for it now."

The building was eerily empty and quiet. Their voices echoed in the lobby. On the elevator to the fourth floor, a silence descended on the family that didn't break until they were in the tiled apartment hallway. Mason dropped his bags and ignored Eva telling him to come back and pick it up. Ahead, were the dining table and chairs and the double glass doors. Eva's reflection was caught on the glass. Long-haired and petite, an inch of space separated her and her son. She had an urge to reach out to bridge their gap, but Charlie opened the sliding doors and Mason was gone. The surface of the pool rippled below them.

They ate a snack of crackers. Afterwards, Eva read to Lucy and listened to her husband and son talking and laughing in a low rumble of incomprehensible noise. Once Lucy was asleep, Eva had a long shower. Charlie was snoring lightly when she was finished. She stood watching him from the bedroom door with the hall light on his face. She thought he'd grown thin since he'd come into her restaurant five nights in a row to ask her out. Her body remembered the sinking sensation she had each time he left without saying anything.

"Mason's tired. We should let him sleep," Charlie said the next morning. He was dressed in his beach shorts which showed the sinewy strength of his body and the shocking whiteness of his chest compared to the tan on his face and arms. Lucy had been awake for a while and was impatient to get out. It was agreed that the girls should go to the beach and collect shells while Charlie made lunch and waited for Mason.

Outside, the breeze was surprisingly cool and sent ripples along the pool. They had not seen anyone on their journey downstairs, and there was no sign of life around the pool either. The beach was separated by a small wooden bridge. Eva glimpsed a figure in the distance walking a dog.

After ten minutes of picking up stones and shells on the beach, Eva was shivering with the cold. It would have been better if they were walking fast, but Lucy kept stopping to add to her collection and Eva kept glancing back hoping to see the boys. She was getting hungry. She hadn't bothered with breakfast because Charlie insisted on the picnic, and now she was sorry. Mason liked to sleep and Charlie would get distracted reading Reddit on the phone and sniggering like a boy. To make it worse, Lucy refused to leave the beach until her bucket was full. When finally they were walking back, Lucy got upset when Eva said she'd have to leave the bucket by the back door of the building.

"But I want to show Dad and Mason," she said.

Eva's stomach was growling, and she felt a little lightheaded. She said nothing, but walked fast and Lucy, who had started to whimper, had to run to catch up. She tripped and sent the bucket flying. To comfort her, Eva said she could bring the shells to the apartment door, but she had to leave it outside. In the gym, an elderly man was walking slowly on the treadmill.

On the second floor, a tall woman with grey hair tied back in a bun got into the elevator and glanced at the bucket in Lucy's hand. She wore the blue uniform of a cleaner and Eva thought her too proper for such attire. She reminded Eva of a Manageress in one of the hotels she'd worked in. The manageress had the same pinched look, though this woman's expression might have been caused by the sand Lucy was dragging into the building. She said nothing to the girl however and merely nodded at the two of them. Eva noticed the woman's fingers were long and sturdy and she wore no rings.

"I'm hungry, Mama," Lucy said. She was shivering too. Eva hugged her and promised her as many peanut butter sandwiches as she could eat. The cleaning lady smiled. Eva smiled back and wished she could think of something more to say than 'hello' and 'goodbye'.

She met Charlie and Mason at the apartment door. "We were just leaving," Charlie said.

"It's too late now," Eva said. "We were down there for hours."

She saw Mason in his swimming truck with tossed hair and a dirty face. "Did you let him have chocolate already, before lunch? Did he even have breakfast?"

"Of course he had breakfast."

Eva saw Charlie winking at the boy.

Mason said, "We could go to the beach now."

Both children had their parent's dark hair and Eva's blue eyes, but she noticed Mason stood like his father with his shoulder folded in slightly and his eyes pleading.

"It's too late," Eva said, and ignored the glance Mason gave his father.

They ate their sandwiches and talked about what to do. It was too cold to go back to the beach and they finally decided that Charlie and Mason would have a look around to see if there was a miniature golf course close-by.

"It's weird, don't you think? How empty the place is?" Eva said.

Mason said it wasn't empty, he'd seen a man in the fitness room yesterday, and a couple earlier by the pool. Eva said, "That's hardly crowded Mason. Do you see how big this place is?"

Mason shrugged.

Charlie said it was off season, that's why they decided to come here this week. It was better than fighting for a place by the pool or on the beach.

Eva said, "It was the only week we could get the place." She saw a flash of worry in her husband's eyes, and said, "I don't understand why they would have a cleaning lady when it's empty. Sit up Lucy."

She had fallen down in her chair with peanut butter all over her mouth and some in her hair, while Mason was hunched over his sandwich. The chocolate on his face was now covered by milk. Eva tried not to look at him.

"What cleaning lady?" Charlie asked.

Eva sighed, "The woman in the navy uniform. I met her in the elevator." Eva was hit with the appalling thought of the woman coming to clean this apartment and seeing their things kept neatly in a pile and away from the drawers and wardrobes.

Charlie was gathering the plates.

Eva said, "Will she come in here?"

"Dan never mentioned any cleaning lady."

"Well, he probably forgot to mention it. The woman who cleans his apartment is probably not on his list of priorities."

She turned in her seat. Her husband was rinsing the plates and she saw the dime-sized bald patch on his head and looked away to the double doors and the pool.

With the boys gone, Eva found space in the drawers for their clothes and hid their bags under the bed in case the cleaning lady would come knocking. She and Lucy had started to watch *Happy Feet* when Charlie phoned and said to come to the pool quickly.

Eva saw the blue rubber behind them and thought that they might have gotten a slide for the pool or a blow-up boat for the kids to play in, until the boys stepped out of the way. Lucy whooped and ran to the edge of the pool before Eva shouted at her to wait.

"It's a boat Mama," Lucy said.

"It's a dinghy. What are we supposed to do with that?" Eva grabbed Lucy's hand. "There's hardly enough room to move in there."

Mason looked on the verge of laughter, but he kept it in when Charlie said, "It's not for the pool."

He gestured towards the sea, separated from them by a gate and small bridge and the grainy sand. Eva laughed, though this only lasted a second because she saw the downcast face of her son and the life jackets and motor that had been placed on one of the lounge chairs.

"You're not serious?"

"It's perfect conditions," Charlie said. He was right. The breeze from earlier had died down. There were only a few clouds in the distance. Charlie was pointing to the sea and asking if she saw the island out there. "It's called Shell Island," he said. "It's closer than it looks."

Mason said the motor would have them there within a half hour and they had oars too.

"We aren't going far," Charlie said, "We'll keep the shore in sight the whole time."

"Charlie, come on," she said, "It's a bad idea."

She said the sea was unpredictable and the island was probably a lot further than it looked. Charlie must have guessed that she'd become resolved to their outing by her easy tone, but Lucy was not allowed to go. Eva didn't have the will to fight the two boys, but she wouldn't succumb to Lucy, and she would think of this later, when the clouds drifted over the sea and sent a dark shadow into the apartment. She'd think of how easily she had let Mason go, while she'd clung to Lucy and it would be a hard thing to forgive.

Lucy cried and begged, and Eva tried to comfort her with promises of ice cream and finishing the movie. When Lucy's crying didn't cease, Eva shouted that Charlie never thought anything through, and she was sick of picking up his mess. Her words echoed in the tiled area amid the high empty rise of the building. She saw the bow of her husband's head, before he said, "It wasn't my mess."

She didn't bring up the years he'd worked side-by-side with his father or that she thought it incredible that Charlie didn't know what his father was doing with the investments, but she stiffened with the thought, and he must have seen the hardening in her eyes.

She didn't see them put on their life jackets and lift the dingy from the pool. She didn't know how her husband carried the motor; if it was light enough to hold in his hands or if he'd put it into the dingy. She thought of them wobbling under the size of it and that they wouldn't have been laughing, not like they must have when they first saw the dingy and talked about the surprise they were about to give the girls. They would have been quiet getting to the sea and climbing in. Charlie would eventually have pushed through his hurt. He probably exclaimed about the beauty around them and how big the sea was or started looking out for fish. Maybe they had fishing rods too and they hadn't had the chance to show her, and Charlie threw the line out and winked at Mason and said, "Wait until you see her face when we bring home dinner." Maybe for a while they were able to imagine Eva's delight.

Eva took Lucy out for ice-cream and they walked back by the beach.

"Look at this Mama," Lucy exclaimed, as she ran into the sea and the wave pushed against her and soaked her shorts. Lucy laughed, but Eva's gaze constantly drifted outward where she tried to make out the black dot of the dingy. The day was getting cooler and a new breeze ruffled Eva's hair on their walk back to the apartment. The quiet was getting to Eva. She felt restless with the memory of Mason's face. His mouth had opened and his eyes had widened, on the verge of crying, when she'd screamed at Charlie. She'd wanted to hit Mason then, to shake him and tell him to wake up. Now she kept hoping for his return so she could pull him to her and say sorry. It was hard to sit still and watch the movie with Lucy, yet it was impossible to move away from her daughter's warm body. Eva sat stiff on the couch. When the room darkened, she had a sense that she'd known of the approaching clouds, and had been awaiting them. She felt as if her heart had split open, but it had started to tear the moment she'd left her son and husband by the pool. Without Lucy, she would have folded up on the couch and cried.

On the screen, the penguin was captive. His feet tapped against the ice while people pressed their face against the glass trying to read his message. Eva was by the glass doors staring out at the sea that had turned a murky grey.

"I can't see them," she said. Lucy sat forward on her seat and said, "What Mama?"

Eva said, "I can't see them."

She had Lucy by the hand. They left the penguin dancing and ran out of the apartment. Eva had no idea where she was going. Her need to get away from the grey that was too immense for a small rubber boat propelled her into the hall, where she stood under the scared gaze of her daughter. There must be a manager or an office somewhere. There had to be a person who would know what to do. She took the elevator down to the ground floor with its mirrored walls and thick carpets, and she shouted hello and squeezed Lucy's hand so hard she cried out.

There was no-one around. Eva thought of going outside but it scared her. To feel the rising breeze and the rain would have made her collapse or scream or both. Then she heard a door close. There were two apartments on the ground floor on the other side of the lounge area. Eva ran towards the apartments and saw the cleaning lady in the corridor. The woman's body was half-hidden by the trolley. Her expression showed no surprise or alarm, but a guarded curiosity when Eva stopped beside her. "They went out on a boat and I can't see them."

"Slow down," the woman said. She smiled at Lucy, and asked Eva who went on a boat and where they'd gone to.

Eva told her about the dingy and the woman said, "There's an empty unit on the sixth floor, you'll be able to see from there. I'm sure it'll be okay."

In the elevator, they didn't talk. The woman glanced at them every now and again and nodded. While Eva wished the woman would say something, to ask questions and ease the tension that surrounded her and her daughter, Eva couldn't bring herself to speak.

The apartment was empty of furniture and had soundless wooden floors that were cool on Eva's bare feet. The back wall was made of glass. Eva would have been stunned with the view and expanse of sky, had her mind not been full with the hope of seeing the boat. She'd run to the window thinking that maybe she'd see her husband close to shore or dragging the boat in, and for a moment, the expectation had felt like reality. She searched the shore line three times before she could admit that they were not there.

Her daughter was behind her, but Eva didn't look at her when the woman unlocked the glass doors. Eva stepped into the rain. The railings were cold. She heard the door closing behind her, but was not alarmed. The woman would not have wanted the rain to get onto the wooden floor. These thoughts were vague in Eva's mind, more a drifting sensation, while she searched for the boat and the island her husband had pointed to. She found nothing and was soaked by the time she went back into the apartment.

"Lucy!" she shouted, and a sense of overwhelming emptiness made her dart further into the room and call her daughter's name again. She was starting to cry when she heard Lucy say, "Mama."

She appeared from the hall holding the woman's hand.

"Did you see them?" the woman asked.

Eva said no. Nerves were making her shaky and lightheaded. She wanted to know where they'd gone and why the woman had taken Lucy away, but the words were caught up in her stomach. Besides, Lucy was with her now, pulling at her arm and asking if she was okay. "We need to go back to the apartment," Eva said to the woman, "I left my phone and someone might have called."

There were no missed calls. Eva changed from her wet clothes and had started to look through the phone book when her phone ringing made her jump. She cried when she heard her husband's voice. They'd stayed too long on the island and the motor had stopped working. They'd tried to row but they went around in circles. No matter how hard they worked, they could not get any closer to the shore. Someone saw them; someone in one of the tall apartments who had looked out the window. Maybe they saw them seconds before Eva looked out, or while Eva was running down to the ground floor and they'd called the Coast Guard.

Eva and Lucy drove to collect them. In the station house, she found them wrapped in blankets. Mason stood and she ran to him and held him. Charlie smiled weakly at Lucy whose arms went around him. She held his hand and led him out after his wife and son.

They had three days left of their holiday in the apartment, but they cut it short when Mason refused to go to the beach. Eva heard him telling Lucy how scary it was to go around in circles and not be able to see the shore. The wind had made them topple over in the dingy more than once and he was sure he would fall out.

Charlie cried in the shower with the water running. Eva opened the door and closed it without saying a word. He might have heard the click of the door closing, because afterwards, his quiet grew around Eva. He would attempt to liven up for his kids. He'd sweep from the bedroom, where he had held his head in his hands, to the living room where he'd clap his hands and say, "What fun will we have today?"

"I don't know, Dad," Mason would say.

Eva said nothing about the guilt she'd felt for letting Mason go, or the time she'd spent running around the building looking for help, or the minutes she'd stood in the rain unable to admit that she couldn't see them. She said, "You shouldn't have done it. You take too many chances."

She felt some victory with his lack of argument. He could finally admit his fault for trusting that man in the store who'd told him the boat was safe and for trusting his own father.

Eva was three weeks back in the office and Charlie had started to work longer hours, when Izzy's head popped up from the cubicle beside her, and said, "It was Marco Island you went to, wasn't it? I knew there was something bad. Come look."

Eva thought about saying she was busy but she sighed and got up.

"What is…?" Eva's voice dropped when she saw the cleaning lady's face with the same quizzical gaze that looked colder in the photo and a little distant, as if the woman had made some judgement towards the photographer.

"She murdered a neighbor and disappeared for a few years. They found her on Marco Island. She was going in and out of people's apartments, imagine that? God."

Izzy turned towards Eva. "Isn't that where you have an apartment?"

Eva shook her head. She said no, it was her husband's boss' place. Izzy frowned, and said that she was sure Eva said they owned it, but Eva wasn't listening. She remembered the sound of the sliding doors closing between her and her daughter, and those long seconds when she'd stood in the rain and the woman held her daughter's hand.

"Are you okay?" Izzy asked. Eva didn't answer. She was beginning to tremble and had to get away from the woman's face. She looked cruel and amused as if she was laughing at Eva. Eva had never asked Lucy what had happened in those minutes, or where they had gone. Now, she wondered what would have happened if she'd waited in the rain a second longer, if she hadn't called to Lucy.

She nearly fell going down the stairs and had to hold onto the bannister. The trembling was all over. In her car, she started the engine and realized she had no idea where to go. Charlie had stopped leaving notes with the address of the houses he was working on. It took two attempts to dial his number. He answered quickly.

"Eva, is everything okay?"

She wanted to tell him about the woman. She wanted to say she was sorry, she didn't know, but couldn't speak with the memory of those glass doors, and her daughter standing behind them.

ANNIVERSARIES

ON FEBRUARY 2ND 2000, Nick Moody was found at the back of the local pub with his head smashed in. Nollaig never forgot the date because of the effect the whole affair had on her daughter. Margaret had been working the night Nick was killed, and after all this time, it was still shocking for Nollaig to think of her girl alone in the place while the assault was going on. Nollaig imagined she would have been vacuuming the red carpet, ridding it of ash and fallen cigarettes, while outside Nick was being beaten. Beside the pub, the river would have gushed forward. It would have been loud that year because of the extra floods. With the vacuum and the water's roar, Nick's shouts would have gone unheard. When Nollaig thought of this, she imagined her daughter humming some tune as she worked, though Margaret had never done such a thing. The girl was too quiet and unassuming.

Since that night, the pub had been refurbished with a

patio in the back with a view of the river; though Nollaig had not set foot inside for years. She couldn't help blame that place for the loss of her daughter.

When Margaret first left, Nollaig couldn't stand being in her house. She kept expecting Margaret to burst through the front door. The constant listening for her daughter's arrival was worse than the silence. She thought she'd get some comfort in her daughter's room. The pink bedspread covered her double bed and cuddly toys lined the walls, but patches on the walls from lost posters made her feel her heart had been ripped from her.

Nollaig grabbed her coat and left the house with no idea where she'd go. By the time the door closed, her gaze was fixed on Eilish Hurley's house across the green with grey smoke issuing from the chimney. When Eilish opened the door, Nollaig was still breathless from the run.

"I just needed to get out of the house for a bit."

Eilish didn't say 'of course, come in'. She didn't say that she knew what it was like to feel an absence. She merely nodded and led Nollaig to the kitchen in the back. Net curtains hung on the window by the sink. There was a smell of roast cooking and a boiling pot on the cooker. The back door was open and three stray cats were feeding on some chicken skin. The sight surprised Nollaig and made her stall at the kitchen door. "You like cats?" she asked.

Eilish was filling the kettle and said, "I don't like throwing food away." She turned off the tap and Nollaig told her that Margaret had left early that morning. It was hard not to cry. She focused on the black cat scratching his back on the ground outside. The cat had his legs in the air and Nollaig viewed it as obscene. Nollaig waited for Eilish to say something. She was a tall, broad-shouldered woman, who was inclined to wear heavy grey sweaters over black leggings, and shawls when outside. Margaret had been on the heavy side too. 'Big-boned' people liked to say, because she didn't seem to have a choice one way or the other, but Eilish had been slimmer once. It was hard for Nollaig to remember her as young. She had a way of looking at you that seemed to come with age, not quite bitter, but wary, and Nollaig felt it now. She stood straighter. A small woman, she felt dwarfed in the gloomy kitchen. A cat meowed.

"Do you want to sit down?" Eilish asked.

Nollaig did.

"They still don't know who did it," Eilish said. "There's no wonder she had to go, always feeling that there was someone over your shoulder."

Eilish didn't say anything about her having to go all the way to Australia. She didn't mention the fact that Margaret could have gone to Dublin or England, though Nollaig felt the query in the room. She'd put a similar question to Margaret.

"It's not about you," Margaret told her, "it's everyone else."

Eilish put the tea on the table and invited Nollaig to stay for dinner. Her son Raymond was on the late shift in the factory, and she didn't like to eat alone. Nollaig was happy to accept. In the following years, she'd visit Eilish most days, but she rarely ate with Eilish when Raymond worked the 8-4 p.m. factory shift. It hurt to come into the house and see the son and mother together; the way Raymond had of smiling at his mother's back or the mother's insistence on filling his plate two and three times were intimacies Nollaig preferred not to see. Besides, she felt that Eilish liked that time alone with her son because for two weeks when he worked nights and evenings, she'd be home from work after Raymond was gone and she hardly saw him. Eilish rarely went to Nollaig's house, and Nollaig thought it was the cats, more than Raymond that kept Eilish at home.

Whenever Margaret wrote, Nollaig would go to Eilish with the letter. She would sit at the table with her tea and tell her of the news.

"She got a job in a café and has to get up at 6 a.m. I never saw her do that in my life," she'd say, and Eilish would make a comment about hard work doing her some good. "Raymond takes overtime in the factory any chance he gets. Last week, he slept five hours before going in again."

"She's still living in the hostel after a year. Wouldn't you think she'd find a nice place? But she says she likes having people around. She feels safer."

"Rent is expensive these days," Eilish would say. "Sure, look at Raymond."

"She's decided to do a secretarial course," Nollaig told her.

Margaret was gone three years at this stage, and the letters had lost their power of excitement. Nollaig was being told of her daughter's life, but couldn't feel it. She wondered what Margaret looked like now and asked for photos, which never came. The year Margaret started in an office; Raymond became the rent collector for the estate. With the new responsibility, Nollaig noticed he started to walk with a straighter back and he smiled more. When he came into the kitchen in the afternoon, he didn't seem to drift.

Nollaig wondered how Margaret was changing on the other side of the world. Was she becoming a different woman?

It was getting harder to go into her daughter's room. She felt raw gazing at the familiar furnishing, where once she'd snuggled beside her daughter, reading stories, or holding her while she slept. Nollaig wanted to imagine Margaret as the little girl who stood shyly on the sideline of the green watching the other children play, but just as her daughter's smells had disappeared from the room, it was impossible to hold onto that little girl.

A little before 2 p.m. on that Sunday, Nollaig put on her coat. There was a temptation to stay at home, but she walked across the green to Eilish's house. The front door was unlocked. In the hall, there was the smell of roasting chicken. Nollaig's hands were empty. Last night, she thought she'd go to the shop for an apple tart and cream, but she hadn't been able to face anyone.

"I didn't see you at mass." Eilish said. She was at the sink peeling potatoes.

Its Nick Moody's anniversary, Nollaig wanted to say, but didn't. The meager winter light seeped through the net curtain and was mostly blocked by Eilish's figure. Eilish never realized it was getting dark. She'd be in the kitchen cooking or cleaning and wouldn't notice the time pass, until she could hardly see in front of her.

Eilish said, "I don't like the new priest Fr. O'Leary. He talks too fast and his whole sermon was about church finances and opening our purses. He said nothing about those young kids."

"The McDonagh's?" Nollaig asked.

"Not just them, there's a gaggle of them causing trouble."

She threw the potato in the pot beside her and Nollaig turned on the light.

"Marie Flanagan's boy is one of them too. Yesterday, I saw him kicking a dog. It looked like a stray but that doesn't make it right. I won't repeat what he said when I told him to stop."

Nollaig said, "Fr. Divine would have said something. He used to thrive on that sort of thing."

Eilish paused in her work to look askance at Nollaig, who had started to cut the potatoes into smaller pieces. There was no point telling Eilish that potatoes would take years to cook whole. She wasn't inclined to listen.

Eilish said, "He had a social conscience. He'd have talked with the parents about their children's behavior."

Nollaig said, "The parents are just as bad, they let them stay out till all hours."

"What are we supposed to be paying him for? If he wants money, he'd better start doing his job," Eilish said.

Nollaig shrugged. A cat meowed. A thin ragged orange cat and a larger white one were eating scraps. Sometimes a small brown cat would appear too. Always, there was a black cat with a splash of white on one paw.

Nollaig said that Eilish should name it, "It's yours, whether you like it or not." But Eilish wouldn't hear of it. She thought certain things can't be owned, like a cat, or grief. But Nollaig owned her grief. She held it to her, and on a certain day every year, she examined it.

She said, "Margaret's been gone nearly five years now."

Eilish nodded, "I don't like the thought of them getting hurt. A cat is a lot smaller than a dog."

Nollaig followed her gaze to the black cat sitting on the backdoor step. There was the distant sound of kids shouting.

After a moment, Eilish said, "You're due a letter from her any day now."

Nollaig said she was due one alright. Eilish might have smiled, but Nollaig's attention was fixed on the sleek body of the cat. He was a beautiful cat, she realized, but only after Eilish arrived at her house to tell her he was gone.

The cat had been missing for two days. Eilish's voice was steady when she said this, but Nollaig recognized the fear in her eyes and thought this was what she must look like every day, but people didn't delve far enough to see it. Eilish said she'd already looked around her side of the estate. Her neighbors hadn't seen him since Monday.

The other side of the estate, where the McDonagh's lived was separated by a patch of green. The McDonagh children, a boy and girl, aged around 15 and 13 were hanging out in front of the house when Nollaig drove home from work earlier, but the street was empty now.

Mrs. McDonagh opened the door. She was a tall, thin

woman with sharp features. From inside, there was the sound of laugher and a playful scream. Nollaig smelt cabbage. Eilish asked if a black cat was seen around here. Mrs. McDonagh's eyes narrowed.

"What are we being blamed for now?" she said.

"Nothing. My cat's missing."

"And I suppose you've asked everyone else in the estate."

When Eilish didn't reply, Mrs. McDonagh's said, "I didn't think so," and closed the door.

Eilish had grown pale. She was probably considering whether or not to knock on that door again. Nollaig imagined her staying there as the light dwindled, determined to get some answers, and was glad she was there to pull Eilish away.

They followed the path past more houses with wooden fences and empty gardens. Near the main road, there was a field. At one time, two benches had been cemented into the middle of the field. The seats were broken and the grass grew long around the cement. Between the field and the river, there was a gravel lane that led to an old graveyard. The two women walked along the path to the graveyard that was surrounded by a stone wall. Years ago, Nollaig had found Margaret smoking there and had been more concerned with the shifting loose rocks than the cigarette. She was thinking of this, and of all the simple things that had once concerned her when Eilish started to walk faster. Nollaig froze in the laneway, watching the bulk of her friend increase speed and stop at the wall. She was bending down as if to kiss the grey stone. Then Nollaig saw the black body. In Eilish's hands, the cat was limp. The paws hung down; on one was a white mark.

Eilish didn't cry, at least not in front of Nollaig. She wrapped the cat in her coat, but not before Nollaig could see the blood. They were quiet as they walked back to the house. At home, Eilish murmured her thanks and said it was okay, she'd take care of him from here. She never mentioned what she did with the body, and no one admitted to hurting the cat. Fr. O'Leary spoke about the cruelty at Mass the next Sunday, but little came of it.

The next time Nollaig went to Eilish's house, she saw the back door was closed. Margaret's last letter arrived a week later. Nollaig sat at her kitchen table for an hour, and thought of all the things people kept inside, like the grief for a cat, and questions about a certain night.

'What did you do?' There were times when Nollaig had wanted to ask her daughter this. But she couldn't because there was too much to lose in the answer. It was impossible that Margaret could have left a man bloody on the ground, and then gone back into the pub to turn off all the lights before going home. Maybe, she'd stood in her dripping wet clothes at Nollaig's bedroom door and debated whether or not to wake her. In her sleep, Nollaig might have been aware of her daughter's presence. She might have been prescient of all those restless nights to come, and tossed and moaned. If she'd managed to wake that night, what would her daughter have said?

Nollaig wanted to believe that it was not her daughter's fault. She wanted to think that Nick had been aware of her habit of stepping outside every night and in his drunken state, he'd thought to take advantage of a woman alone. Yet, this image of him never remained. Instead, she imagined the call of nature that took him around the corner, on his way home from whatever woman he'd been with, and his form diminished by the rain.

It was dark when she started for Eilish's house with the letter in hand. She needed to talk to someone but had no idea what she would say. At home, she imagined telling Eilish that it was impossible to be happy with the good news of her daughter's return, after what happened to the cat. She should be thrilled, but instead she was worried about Margaret's safety here.

She imagined saying aloud, "I keep thinking of people lurking with rocks ready to hurt the first defenseless thing that comes their way."

She thought Eilish would probably nod and ask if she wanted some tea.

Green Balloons

For my son's fifth birthday party, we blew up balloons in the kitchen and every time we found a green one, I had to go outside and let it go. The first time I ran out, my son ran after me. In the back yard, he frowned and asked why I did that. I couldn't begin to explain so I told him it was fun and he should try it. His balloon was red. He let it go and laughed. It was a bright day with a wind that made the balloons dance. The second time I found a green one he said 'Mama' and his voice was small. He stayed by the back door, holding his balloon close, while mine went high. I had to shield my eyes from the sun to watch it. The third time he said 'Mama no.'

When the party was over, I texted you to say that my son stopped me from letting any more green balloons go. He insisted they were his favorite color, just like you.

I got a reply; *my favorite color is not green and who are you anyway?*

❋

I am still the girl you approached in the school canteen years ago. I tried to ignore you, but you were never one to be ignored. You stood across from me, for how long? One minute, a few seconds? It was impossible to tell and a relief when you finally said, "Hi, I'm Natalie."

I looked up to see a thin girl in jeans and a sweater. Dark hair fell over your face and your shoulders folded inward, though there was nothing shy about you. You were just light enough to blow away.

"You're new aren't you?"

I nodded. You had to ask my name before I told it.

"Lisa, that's pretty. Can I sit?"

You didn't wait for an answer.

"So what's up, are you depressed?"

I'd spent three days in a psychiatric hospital and had hardly spoken since, so I would have said yes, if I'd felt like talking. Your eyebrows rose up in the way I would get used to. The gesture could mean, 'this is a fucking joke', as it did in group therapy; or 'way to go,' as it did when I phoned my mother and lied about extra work so we could hang out; or 'seriously, is that it?' as it did when I offered nothing.

It's hard to imagine who I'd be if you'd given up, but you didn't. You rested your chin on hands that lay flat on the table. Your upward gaze made you look impish. You said, "If you could be any animal, what would it be?" You didn't wait for a response before you said, "I'd be a sloth, just hanging out in the trees all day with no one bothering me. There's something in the leaves that gets them stoned. Did you know that?"

You said, "They're so chilled they only shit once a week… ha you smiled."

After a pause, you asked, "What about you?"

I thought of a bird straight away, white with a huge wingspan, I didn't know what it was, probably something I made up.

"I bet you'd like to be a horse," you said.

You were on the far side of the table, but you were reaching inside me too. I could feel the pull of words, *why a horse?* It was the first time I'd been curious in weeks.

"Yeah, a horse," you said pleased with yourself.

I was fifteen and had just moved with my family to Gardner, Massachusetts. Before the move, we'd never heard of the Pace School. I was supposed to go to the local high school. My parents kept my name on the list for the first six months of that year. They phoned to tell the principal we were delayed and would not be moving until April. I imagined them sneaking around town trying to pretend they weren't there so they could pretend I wasn't walking around a school where group therapy was part of the curriculum.

I don't think they were ashamed as much as shocked and off-balance. For a while, a stranger had lived in their house. I'd broken glasses and plates and screamed about the unfairness of leaving everything I knew. Then the rage left as suddenly as it came and I didn't want to get out of bed. Mom would sit beside me and say, "Lisa please, you have to eat," and I'd stare at nothing and think if I opened my mouth I would be swallowed by myself, like when you fold the sock inward. When I was left alone, my mouth would open and close. No matter how many times I did it, I was still on the bed, so one day I opened my mouth and swallowed all the aspirin I could find.

"It's the move," the doctors told my parents. "It's caused a lot of anxiety."

My mother wouldn't stop apologizing after that and I hated her for making my sorrow her own. It was always her fault, her grievance, her regret. You were the only one I told, and you said, "But isn't that what Moms do?"

I said, "What?"

You said, "Get it wrong."

Yours didn't. She was sweet, but you didn't want sweet. You wanted someone to knock the thoughts out of your head.

"I've made a friend," I told my mother after my first day at Pace.

She was skeptical until she met you. She thought we would bring each other down, like a person drowning can drag the rescuer to the bottom.

I said, "What if we are rescuing each other?" No, I didn't, but I wish I did. I didn't know what to say and then you came running out of the school. It was a bright day. I remember how pale your skin looked, luminous, an angel running towards us. You stopped breathless. The keys in my Mom's hand jingled; a sign of nervousness.

"Hello, Lisa's mom."

Mom glanced at me and then at you standing with your hand out and I saw the ice thaw.

"You must be Natalie," she said, "I've heard a lot about you."

You nodded and said, "Which one?"

I laughed but my mother frowned. You apologized and said it was a bad joke. She asked me in the car what you meant. I said I didn't know because I didn't want to explain.

Another day you said, "My favorite color's green, not the light green that people turn when they're about to get sick, like my Mom when she had to visit me in hospital. I'm talking dark green, like those pictures of the Amazon that are taken from the sky."

"Yellow," I said, though that surprised me.

You said, "Lithium is yellow. Trintellix is yellow too."

"Or they're pink."

You said, "Yeah I never liked pink. Clonidine is light green."

I asked what that was for.

"Anxiety, panic attacks. It keeps my head quiet."

I said, "My head's too quiet. It's like the radio without stations."

"With the fuzzy shit?"

"Not even the fuzzy shit."

"I want your head," you said.

✳

"Come on, let's explore," you used to say.

"Explore what?"

"Exactly," you'd say and you'd drag me down the school's corridors, to peek into rooms and I couldn't stop laughing even as I said, "No, don't."

✳

When I left Gardner I texted you about my parent's messy divorce. In college, I texted *and here am I budding among the ruins,* after reading the poem, because that was me after you.

I texted you when I started working with teenagers in the recreational center and about my guilt for looking for you in every face, which eventually turned to disappointment, and then to seeing the kids for who they were.

After I met Mike, I texted to say you'd like him. I told you he was an architect and drew cartoons. The first thing I noticed was his smile. It was easy to be with him, like being with you.

I told you about my son.

Mike saw that text. "I didn't know you were scared," he said.

I sat on the bed beside him. Our son was asleep in his cot. Outside someone was mowing the lawn. A picture of domesticity. I was scared; every time I looked at my son's face I felt tiny. I didn't know if I was ready for it. It was so fucking huge.

He held me close to him, and said, "I'm the one here, Lisa, you should talk to me, not her."

On our son's fifth birthday, my husband found me crying in the bedroom. The television was on downstairs releasing a blare of cartoons. He sat by me and asked what was wrong.

When I showed him the text, he kissed my forehead and said, "You need to erase her number."

I leaned deeper into him. I would have liked to disappear.

"Jake told me about the green balloons," he said and I heard the worry in his voice.

I didn't want to ask what Jake said because I didn't want to know.

I said, "Natalie loved plants. Her green fingers were one thing she was sure of. She watered them up to the last minute. She had us fooled."

I remember some mornings you laid your pills out on your kitchen table and your long fingers were so graceful. I loved watching you.

"How do I know you'll never try to hurt yourself again?" You asked.

I said, "Because I won't, I promise."

You said me too, and every day, we'd text that single word, *'promise'*.

Our last year of school, we fought on the phone. You told me you wanted me to leave you alone. You said it was hard work trying to keep me happy. I said that I'd never asked anything from you and you said everyone wants something. Years later, my son would wake with an earache. He'd bawl until the painkiller kicked in and then he'd lie sleeping with his face pressed against mine. His breathing would remind me of you because of the way it entered some part of me and stayed for a long time.

After a long pause, you said, "I'm sorry but I can't keep doing this. There's so much in my head and it hurts. I just want it to be quiet."

You hung up and my hands shook when I texted, 'Promise.'

You didn't text back. I phoned your mother and told her she needed to go home now. She needed to stop you.

I remember your mother in a long skirt and a white blouse. I remember her hair falling over her face, but I don't remember if she was in the house that day, if she rushed from her office or had to leave her trolley half-filled with food in the middle of an aisle. These small missing details get to me sometimes. It's like having a picture with parts uncolored. When I ask her, she says it doesn't matter, but I know she burst into your room and screamed before she ran to you.

The second time we met in a canteen, it was not at school but in the hospital. I sat opposite you and you asked how I managed to keep my promise and be the visitor, not the patient. I had to wait until I got outside before I cried because my tears would only have made you feel worse. I told you that I'd tried to make a reservation to stay with you, but they were booked up and you smiled.

I wasn't as good at making people laugh as you were. You had bruises on your neck that I wanted to touch. I wanted to ask you questions that would draw you out; if you could go anywhere where would it be? If you could meet anyone who would it be? But I was frightened of what you might say.

You were angry at me and didn't know whether or not to forgive me for phoning your mother. "Why did you do it?"

I said because you were my best friend and I love you. I didn't want to lose you.

"I can't explain what it was like, the panic in those minutes before Mom came when I felt myself drifting away." You were crying. "I'm afraid to do it again and I hate you for doing that to me."

Your phone stayed off when you came home. When my mother drove me to school, she parked the car instead of leaving me at the drop off area. She'd squeeze my hand while I watched the kids going into the building waiting for a glimpse of your dark hair. I know my mother cried those mornings while she watched me go into school alone.

I called your mother and asked what was going on.

She said, "Don't worry, she's doing okay. She took a walk today. I think she went shopping, and she's watering the plants."

I think of you planning it all out slowly, just like you used to lay out your pills. The hat would have been your first buy.

I have an image of you in your big coat at that end of summer heat. It should have made us laugh. Afterward, we should have gone into your house and taken it off, so you would become again the slight girl I knew.

In the canteen, you said you hated me and then you said you were sorry. You sang, 'I'm just a kid with depression, anxiety, bipolar too, how about you?' And I laughed. But you were warning me. You said you were too afraid to do that again. You didn't say you didn't want to do it again. Now I listen to every word the kids in the center say.

You seemed happy that morning. Your mother said you had breakfast, talked and smiled and helped her do the dishes, but by that stage you'd already phoned 911.

I was in school when the police started for your house. I was either walking to class or staring out the window when your mother realized you weren't in your room.

She found you in the garage wearing the winter coat and your hair tucked under a baseball cap. She asked what you were doing and you told her it would be okay. I was probably watching the clock in the classroom, seeing the seconds slip by, when she ran into the kitchen to phone your doctor on the same line you'd used only half an hour earlier when you pleaded for the police to hurry. You probably said, "He has a gun, hurry please."

Your mother was told to stay on the line. "Can you please hold?"

She said yes. She said she didn't see you leave the garage with your coat, a school bag strapped to your back and a toy gun in your hand. "There was noise," she said. She heard the cars, but she didn't know something was wrong until she heard the man shout. She said she couldn't move. It was as if her heart had turned to ice. The shot made her drop the phone and she ran to the front door. Then she screamed and didn't stop screaming for a long time.

That first day you said, "Yeah, bet you'd be a horse."

I leaned towards you and said, "Can I be a bird?"

You smiled and said, "Yeah awesome, stay up in the trees with me."

I couldn't erase your number. I asked Mike to do it. He took the phone from me and I said, "No wait. I need to write one more thing."

I wrote that when the kids first come to the center, I ask them what animal they would like to be. Even the ones with nothing to say answer.

I pressed send. Before I deleted the number, I got a text.

A cat, the person on the other end answered.

Games They Played

Raindrops pummeled Joan's window and made her toss and turn. She would not have slept regardless, because of the image of her husband's hands on another woman's body. He'd phoned from the pub to tell Joan he was going to her. He'd said, "I need to tell her the truth."

She'd pleaded with him not to go. There had been a pause, and then he'd said he had to go, and hung up. She'd immediately started to call the Dun Maeve Pub, but didn't dial the last number. She would not be the wife phoning for her husband, the wife on the line waiting while the big sullen bargirl walked slowly to him. She might shout, "Hey Nick, for you," though she seemed a woman disinclined to shout or hurry. Joan didn't want that girl to say her husband's name aloud, so she hung up and sat in the kitchen, until the clock told her it was 2 a.m. Then she went to bed.

Her husband might have been with her as she tossed and

turned, and grew angrier and angrier. He wouldn't have been on the bed, lying behind her back, as she'd felt often since, but on the chair by the window watching her with the shadows from the rain on his face. The Guards said he was killed anywhere between 1a.m. and 3 a.m. In those first hours, he would have kept a distance, because he wouldn't have wanted to scare her. Maybe he would have said her name, Joan, Joanie. He might have been with her at 5 a.m. when she went downstairs in her robe, feeling the air on her bare thighs and thinking of his hand on *her* thighs? Sally. She lived on Station Road, Sally Lawlor; her name was in the phone book. Joan stared at it for a long time.

"Fuck you Nick," she'd said to the empty room. "This is not what we're supposed to do."

She would have screamed this if not for the kids sleeping, Shane 3 and Laura, 5. They'd been restless through the night. Shane had woken for the babysitter and it had taken a while before he'd fallen back to sleep. The babysitter might have wondered why Joan had come home alone. The young girl might have realized that the couple had argued and Joan was not happy. When she looked in the mirror after the sitter had gone, she saw her mouth was a thin line and her jaw was tight. She cursed him in the bathroom while changing out of her wet clothes. She cursed him while walking the stairs, dialing the pub, and looking for Sally's number, and when the rain finally eased and his side of the bed was cold and empty, she cursed him. He might have been there and she didn't notice, not like she would later.

Or, he might have been stuck outside. Sometimes, she imagined him standing outside their house with rain falling down his hair and face. She never pictured him with injuries to his head. She couldn't think of him bloody and torn, but only as she last saw him, with his dark hair falling over his forehead and his gaze dropping too quickly from her.

Through rain drenched glass, he might have seen her carry their son down-stairs and put him in his chair by the table. Her husband might have reached out with a hand that could no longer touch, towards the cool glass and the sight of his daughter, Laura, coming down the stairs minutes later. And he might have seen the garda car drive up to the house. The sun had come out by then and the green of their garden glistened. The car tires went through puddles and gave a swishing sound in the still neighborhood of white, two-story houses with small front lawns. Early Sunday, some families were getting ready for mass. Some may have seen the car pull up in front of Joan's house. There were those minutes when she fed Shane, got breakfast for Laura, drank her coffee and glanced at the clock over and over. She'd do anything to get those minutes back, and be again that woman who was angry rather than grief-stricken and guilty; to be that woman, who didn't recognize the feel of her husband in the room with a shift in the air so slight, it was like the ruffle of a feather; or the sense of pressure on her back when she slept. She'd go back to the woman who turned towards the ringing doorbell with a look of irritation. She didn't take Shane with her. She let him climb from the chair and go with Laura to the living room. In a flash of little limbs and skin, the children disappeared into the room just before she opened the front door. They would never be those children again. They would come out of the room different, but she didn't know that then.

This is what she thought—she thought her husband told Sally the truth, and she freaked out and kicked him out into the rain. Nick, being Nick, never one to turn away from the wounded, would have tried to get back into the house.

Joan thought he's in fucking trouble now and it's his own fault. She answered the door livid, and that anger didn't leave when she saw the faces of the man and woman, one stocky, the other thin. Both had eyes full of pity. Their unease was felt in the pause. They had to ask to be allowed in, and she should have kept quiet. She should have bit her tongue, stepped back and said nothing, but she'd been awake all night. She'd been thinking of him with Sally for hours, and she couldn't keep it in. She said, "He's been with her all night."

Or it might have been, "I fucking know he was with her all night." She may have cursed. It was one thing she couldn't remember afterwards-what she'd said. She remembered only that it was about Sally and that she sounded like the bitter, angry wife. It must have been at that moment that her husband drifted into the house. She felt something then; a chill start on her skin, and a fear more than unease made her want to shut the door on her visitors and lock herself in. But she didn't move and they had to ask again if they could come in. It was a blur what happened once they were in the kitchen, but on the way there, she shivered. This she recalls because it happened a lot after. A shiver would rise from deep inside her and feel like it was his hand reaching into her.

Before she'd got to the kitchen, she was regretting what she'd said. Now she believed it was why he stayed. He stayed not because of the violence of his death, or because his killer was still out there roaming free, though they questioned Sally's ex-husband, he was not charged for lack of evidence. Her husband stayed because Joan had spoken about him in such a manner, and because she had not taken it back. She had not told anyone what really happened—that after their second child was born, Joan couldn't bear to be touched. Her baby had pulled that part of her out, so she'd felt hollow inside. Her skin had felt too thin and light, too sensitive to touch, not painful as much as fearful with the idea that she could be erased further, that her soul was too close to the surface. It wasn't post-natal depression; at least she didn't think so. She had energy for her children. She liked the garden. She liked to walk. Everything seemed okay, except when she was alone with her husband. She felt something of that sensation still; an unease deep inside her and a desire to flee the room when she felt his presence, though her Nick deserved more from her, because there was *her* Nick, and then there was the Nick Moody people talked about, the adulterer. She knew she had made the second one, and yet she'd said nothing to defend him.

Not long ago, Joan's mother had come to the house. She'd stood at the kitchen door with her coat still on her slight frame, and she'd said, "Is it true?"

Joan said, "Please Mom, don't."

And her mother had hugged her, though Joan's arms had hung limply by her side. She'd been afraid of her urge to push her mother away and shout at her that she had it wrong, that Nick was not who they said he was. Joan had often caught her mother staring at the photos on the wall, as if she didn't know the man in them. In the kitchen, near the door was a family portrait taken when Shane was nearly two. He was a young dark-haired boy who couldn't sit still, and Nick was behind him. They had the same eyes and hair. His arm was around his son's waist, their daughter Laura was on Joan's knees. They were all smiling. Nick was leaning towards Joan, who had days before, after two years, finally opened to him. All because of the party and Nuala O'Grady in her short dress, who had stood talking to Nick for a long time. She'd leaned in towards him and whispered to him over the loud music. Joan, watching, had imagined the feel of her breast rubbing against his arm. Later at home, with the babysitter gone and the house ticking around them, their children sleeping soundly in bed, she'd studied her husband and asked if Nuala had turned him on. He'd been shocked at first and had denied it. She'd persisted and he must have seen the change in her face, with the warmth seeping through a body that had felt, until that night, too thin to hold any longing. So, he'd told her yes. He'd whispered what he would have liked to do to Nuala, and Joan had moaned under him.

Afterward, in the dark, she'd said, "I want you to go to her and then come back and tell me everything."

He said he would never do that, but the next morning, she'd slid out of bed when his arm went around her. The hurt was worse than all the times before, because she'd revealed herself to him and now she was concealed again.

Nuala wasn't the first girl he went to. She was too close to them. They were careful at the beginning. Sally had been a mistake.

Joan rose and tossed the coffee in the sink. She was sure she saw a shadow on the window, a flitter of movement, there and gone. It was a dark, dull day, with clouds that hung low on the ground. The kids were at pre-school and school. The house buzzed with the quiet, and Joan grabbed her car keys and went to the car without bothering with a jacket. Sally lived on Station Road, on the other side of the village. Joan had to drive by the secondary school, where the yards were empty of children, and over the bridge where the river rushed on its way to the sea. The Dun Maeve's front door was locked. She'd seen her husband for the last time in the pub. He'd been quiet. When she'd asked him what was wrong, he'd said he felt bad about what they were doing. He'd stared into his pint and had refused to leave with his wife. She'd wanted to plead with him to come home, but there were too many people, and she wouldn't make a scene. She doubted she would ever set foot in the pub again.

On Station Road, she slowed and took the first left into the estate. Sally's house was a narrow, two-story white house. A bicycle tossed on its side was in the driveway and the curtains were still drawn in the living-room at 10 a.m. Twice, Joan had driven to the house before. Twice, she'd sat in the car and stared at it, unable to knock on the door. It had struck her that she knew what the house was like. She'd stepped inside the front door with Nick and had seen the dark-painted walls and carpeted hall that was so narrow, Nick said he'd felt claustrophobic, and he'd had an urge to leave straight away. Now, Joan wondered if it was the house or Sally that had made him want to flee. Nick told his wife that Sally said nothing, before she took his hand and led him upstairs. Joan had imagined Sally pausing at the door to look at Nick, and had felt an excited lurch in her stomach. Sally had a round sweet face with a small mouth and black hair cut short. Joan had seen her before Nick had. She'd told him there's a woman on Station Road with pretty lips.

How did they meet? She couldn't remember now, though she liked to hear about the first meetings. There was an element of subterfuge in the way Nick approached them, but Nick spoke little of his first encounters with Sally.

Joan parked outside the house, but she couldn't move until she saw Sally at the front door, barefoot in jeans and a t-shirt. Joan thought of driving away, and she imagined Sally would remain in that doorway long after the car had gone.

"I thought you'd come," Sally said, when Joan had gotten to the door.

They looked nothing alike. Sally was smaller and sweet looking; 'warm', Joan would have described her, not beautiful, but pretty and sexy with her full figure. Joan was taller, fairer, and more cool than warm. She wanted to fold into the other woman's softness, as her husband must have done, and she wanted to slap Sally's face, take something of that warmth for herself.

The kitchen was at the back of the house. There was a mess of dishes in the sink. The floor had been swept, but the crumbs and other bits and pieces had been brought to the door and left there. For the first weeks after her husband's death, Joan's house had been a mess too. She'd rise every now and again to tidy some part of it or clean, but she would sit down nearly straight away, having forgotten the cause for her rising or because she was hit with a fatigue that stuck to her bones.

The kitchen was darker than Joan's and smaller, with a round table to the left of the back door. She thought shadows from the low-lying clouds outside would be cast on the table, but saw only a used mug and a plate with crusts left from toast. Sally had walked into the kitchen and then stood in the middle of the room gazing at Joan with a look that was impossible to decipher. She may have been nervous, or defensive, but her body was too open, as if she was expecting a slap. She looked like an offering standing before Joan. There was no mention of sitting, but Joan had to hide herself a little. On the chair by the table, she folded inward. Sally's vulnerability had made Joan protective of herself.

There was no clock in the room. There was stillness of time with the two women; a quiet that got thicker and harder to break the longer it went on. Sally made no offer of tea or water. Joan's mouth and throat were so dry, but she couldn't ask this woman for anything. It was not hate she felt. It might have been easier if it was something like that. Jealousy could be fought against too; the notion that her husband had spent his last night in Sally's arms could have been disarmed by the fact that he was going home to Joan when he'd been struck. But the tenderness Joan felt towards the woman, who had taken the other seat at the table, was debilitating.

"You knew," Sally started and then stopped. Her hands were on the table. Then they weren't, and she was sitting back. She looked as if she didn't know if she wanted to sit or stand, and Joan thought of the police coming here after her house. They would have had less sympathy for the mistress.

"Yes, I knew," Joan said.

Sally nodded. "I'm sorry," she said, and Joan wanted to tell her that she had no reason to be sorry. She wanted to say she should be apologizing for the way she used Sally. In Joan's own house, she'd wanted to be cruel, but in the dim light, she'd been struck dumb. She imagined her husband had lied; that the first night Sally had brought him into this room and not upstairs. He'd sat on the same seat Joan was in now, and he'd fallen in love with Sally by this table. She would have talked to him with her elbows on the table, or she would have sat back and tilted her head and let him talk.

"He was at the back of the pub," Joan said, because she needed to say something and she'd always doubted that he'd been found in the rubble area by the wall. On the other side of the wall, the river was so close, a gushing torrent of water. Sally shook her head and wiped her tears. She said, "He was going home."

Joan knew there were things Sally wasn't saying. She

could see it in the dart of her downward gaze and in the sorrow that emanated from her. Joan felt heavy in the seat, so old suddenly with the realization that her husband was going home, but he didn't want to. He'd walked Station Road and the quiet village street where all the buildings were in darkness and no-one was awake to see him drift by. He'd paused before the bridge and the road that would lead him to his wife. It was raining heavily, but he wouldn't have cared. He'd always loved the river. Was it this that pulled him to the back of the pub, or was it another person, that nameless one who was the last to see her husband alive? It didn't matter.

"I don't know why I came," Joan said.

Sally nodded. She said she was sorry again, and Joan wanted to scream at her to stop saying that. She had a sudden need to get out of the house and away from the woman's sorrow that shouldn't have belonged to her. Joan rose on legs that felt too thin for her body. Sally watched. The upward lift of her head made her look like a child.

"How did you know?" Sally's voice was low, and she'd looked away from Joan seconds after she spoke. Joan felt a hole had opened inside her. She'd wanted to say she knew because it was a game they played, that her husband would come home and tell her everything they'd done. But she wasn't able to find the anger, not when she saw her husband too clearly stopping on that road in the deserted village, prolonging the moments when he would have to face his wife.

"I need to tell her the truth," Nick had said and Joan had

never asked what truth.

Joan said, "It doesn't matter how. You were not the first woman." Maybe Sally knew this already because there was no reaction to the news. She didn't move from her seat while Joan stumbled to the front door and opened it to the cool chill of the air. She felt him then, her husband, a light breath behind her, and she stood for a long time, unsure if she had the strength to step outside.

Acknowledgements

A lucky writer is one who has readers who will help on the journey. I am very forever grateful to the people who are on the sidelines for me. Christy, for always keeping me on the right track and making me question what I mean, Kim, for your attention to detail and patient editing, Jennifer, Gloria and Ryan, for reading first and second drafts, this book wouldn't be the same without you. And a special thank you to Marc and Donna at Fomite for giving my stories a home and for being wonderful to work with.

About Fomite

A fomite is a medium capable of transmitting infectious organisms from one individual to another.

"The activity of art is based on the capacity of people to be infected by the feelings of others." Tolstoy, *What Is Art?*

Writing a review on Amazon, Good Reads, Shelfari, Library Thing or other social media sites for readers will help the progress of independent publishing. To submit a review, go to the book page on any of the sites and follow the links for reviews. Books from independent presses rely on reader-to-reader communications.

For more information or to order any of our books, visit:

http://www.fomitepress.com/FOMITE/Our_Books.html

More Titles from Fomite...

Novels

Joshua Amses — *During This, Our Nadir*

Joshua Amses — *Ghatsr*

Joshua Amses — *Raven or Crow*

Joshua Amses — *The Moment Before an Injury*

Jaysinh Birjepatel — *Nothing Beside Remains*

Jaysinh Birjepatel — *The Good Muslim of Jackson Heights*

David Brizer — *Victor Rand*

Paula Closson Buck — *Summer on the Cold War Planet*

Dan Chodorkoff — *Loisaida*

David Adams Cleveland — *Time's Betrayal*

Jaimee Wriston Colbert — *Vanishing Acts*

Roger Coleman — *Skywreck Afternoons*

Marc Estrin — *Hyde*

Marc Estrin — *Kafka's Roach*

Marc Estrin — *Speckled Vanities*

Zdravka Evtimova — *In the Town of Joy and Peace*

Zdravka Evtimova — *Sinfonia Bulgarica*

Fomite

Fomite

L.E. Smith — *The Consequence of Gesture*

L.E. Smith — *Travers' Inferno*

L.E. Smith — *Untimely RIPped*

Bob Sommer — *A Great Fullness*

Tom Walker — *A Day in the Life*

Susan V. Weiss —*My God, What Have We Done?*

Peter M. Wheelwright — *As It Is On Earth*

Suzie Wizowaty — *The Return of Jason Green*

Poetry

Anna Blackmer — *Hexagrams*

Antonello Borra — *Alfabestiario*

Antonello Borra — *AlphaBetaBestiaro*

Antonello Borra — *Fabbrica delle idee/The Factory of Ideas*

L. Brown — *Loopholes*

Sue D. Burton — *Little Steel*

David Cavanagh— *Cycling in Plato's Cave*

James Connolly — *Picking Up the Bodies*

Greg Delanty — *Loosestrife*

Mason Drukman — *Drawing on Life*

J. C. Ellefson — *Foreign Tales of Exemplum and Woe*

Tina Escaja/Mark Eisner — *Caida Libre/Free Fall*

Anna Faktorovich — *Improvisational Arguments*

Barry Goldensohn — *Snake in the Spine, Wolf in the Heart*

Barry Goldensohn — *The Hundred Yard Dash Man*

Barry Goldensohn — *The Listener Aspires to the Condition of Music*

R. L. Green — *When You Remember Deir Yassin*

Gail Holst-Warhaft — *Lucky Country*

Raymond Luczak — *A Babble of Objects*

Kate Magill — *Roadworthy Creature, Roadworthy Craft*

Tony Magistrale — *Entanglements*

Gary Mesick — *General Discharge*

Andreas Nolte — *Mascha: The Poems of Mascha Kaléko*

Sherry Olson — *Four-Way Stop*

Brett Ortler — *Lessons of the Dead*

Aristea Papalexandrou/Philip Ramp — *Μας προσπερνά/It's Overtaking Us*

Fomite

Fomite

Elizabeth Genovise — *Where There Are Two or More*
Andrei Guriuanu — *Body of Work*
Zeke Jarvis — *In A Family Way*
Arya Jenkins — *Blue Songs in an Open Key*
Jan English Leary — *Skating on the Vertical*
Marjorie Maddox — *What She Was Saying*
William Marquess — *Boom-shacka-lacka*
Gary Miller — *Museum of the Americas*
Jennifer Anne Moses — *Visiting Hours*
Martin Ott — *Interrogations*
Christopher Peterson — *Amoebic Simulacra*
Jack Pulaski — *Love's Labours*
Charles Rafferty — *Saturday Night at Magellan's*
Ron Savage — *What We Do For Love*
Fred Skolnik— *Americans and Other Stories*
Lynn Sloan — *This Far Is Not Far Enough*
L.E. Smith — *Views Cost Extra*
Caitlin Hamilton Summie — *To Lay To Rest Our Ghosts*
Susan Thomas — *Among Angelic Orders*
Tom Walker — *Signed Confessions*
Silas Dent Zobal — *The Inconvenience of the Wings*

Odd Birds

William Benton — *Eye Contact: Writing on Art*
Micheal Breiner — *the way none of this happened*
J. C. Ellefson — *Under the Influence: Shouting Out to Walt*
David Ross Gunn — *Cautionary Chronicles*
Andrei Guriuanu and Teknari — *The Darkest City*
Gail Holst-Warhaft — *The Fall of Athens*
Roger Lebovitz — *A Guide to the Western Slopes and the Outlying Area*
Roger Lebovitz — *Twenty-two Instructions for Near Survival*
dug Nap— *Artsy Fartsy*
Delia Bell Robinson — *A Shirtwaist Story*
Peter Schumann — *Belligerent & Not So Belligerent Slogans from the
                    Possibilitarian Arsenal*
Peter Schumann — *Bread & Sentences*

Fomite

Peter Schumann — *Charlotte Salomon*

Peter Schumann — *Diagonal Man Theory + Praxis, Volumes One and Two*

Peter Schumann — *Faust 3*

Peter Schumann — *Planet Kasper, Volumes One and Two*

Peter Schumann — *We*

Plays

Stephen Goldberg — *Screwed and Other Plays*

Michele Markarian — *Unborn Children of America*

Essays

Robert Sommer — *Losing Francis: Essays on the Wars at Home*